SOUL CURSED

GODS CURSED SERIES BOOK 2

LEISL LEIGHTON

PERMIEN PRESS

Published by Leisl Leighton as Permien Press. For more information, email: leisl@leislleighton.com

First published 2021 in the A Perfectly Paranormal Halloween Anthology. Republished 2023 as a single title novella by Permien Press.

Cover design – Samantha Marshall; Editor – Marnie St Clair

eBook ISBN: 978-0-6451089-7-2; Print ISBN: 978-0-6451089-8-9

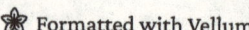 Formatted with Vellum

PRAISE FOR THE GODS CURSED SERIES

I loved the way Leisl Leighton wrote this, it was what I was hoping for in this type of book. The characters were what I was hoping for. I was invested in the plot and really glad I read this.

SOUL CURSED

To Mark — the hero of my story.
This wouldn't have happened without you.

TAMUEL'S CURSE

"You cannot kill this child, witch, for he belongs to me. Of my flesh, I am the only one with the authority to take his life. But as you point out, the Gods' laws dictate that the son will pay for the hubris of the father. I will curse this child's soul, not for your purposes, Clodia, but for mine!

Hear me this day: I bind this child to my service, to be bound more tightly than any other cupid by his cupid powers. He will find love for others in his service, but is never to seek it for himself. Only the cracked piece of his soul's mirror, cursed both equal and opposite, will make him whole and set him free."

Eros to Vestal Priestess-Witch Clodia: as etched into the holy Keeper of the Curses, Revenant of the Eternal Well.

CHAPTER
ONE

Tamuel stumbled on the smooth black floor as the portal closed with a little whoosh behind him. He quickly steadied himself, blinked then glanced down at the chronometer on his wrist. The ancient clockwork dial glowed as it whirred silently. Not too bad. The time difference between the Underworld and the Earthly Realm hadn't shrunk too much as the veil thinned for All Hallows' Eve. He took a breath – time to get on with his quest. It wouldn't do to get caught here.

He looked around, orienting himself. This wasn't quite what he expected the tunnels of the Underworld to look like, but then again, what would he know? It wasn't like there were tourist brochures. Perhaps there should be though. The veins of red, purple and green that ran chaotically along the glossy black rock walls, lighting the space, were quite pretty.

But why was it so warm? He didn't think this part of the Underworld was supposed to have the Fires of Hell – that was a particular quirk only found in the Morningstar's kingdom. Damn – had the portal dumped him in the wrong part of the Hell Realms?

He turned then stilled. He wasn't in tunnels – he stood in what looked like a large lounge room complete with spring-green rug, red upholstered furniture and flowers on every buffet, side table and antique drawers scattered around the room.

Standing in front of a fireplace that looked like it had been hewn by giant teeth, limned by the flickering firelight, were a couple in a lover's embrace.

Not just any couple. Hades and Persephone.

Shit-fuck-damn! What in all the Hells were they doing here? They were supposed to be at Persephone's All Hallows' Eve party.

He must have done something wrong. His spell was supposed to have dropped him right outside Varagustus' cell. It sure as damnation wasn't supposed to drop him into Hades' private lounge room.

This was not at all going to plan.

Thank all the Gods neither Hades nor Persephone had noticed him portal in uninvited. Famous for their displays of PDA, they were currently too wrapped up in their kiss – and in a state of half-undress – to notice him standing near the door. Actually, only Hades was partly undressed. Persephone was obviously in costume for her Halloween party. A quick glance at the broken horns, trident and torn cape that lay on the green rug in front of Hades' throne-like armchair had Tamuel guessing it was the reason they were still here. Hades famously hated dressing up.

What a bloody cock-up! He hadn't taken Hades' mood into consideration when planning this. The Fates must be meddling again – they loved pulling on unexpected threads and watching the chaos that unfolded. He was certain they

4

did it for shits and giggles. He wished there was a way to show them just how not funny their meddling was.

He glanced at his bloody right wrist where the sigil for the portal spell was carved into his skin. Hades and Persephone still being here could ruin everything. He had to find Clodia and get her to tell him what she'd done with his mother's powers. He'd made a vow and it was either succeed or die trying.

He'd prefer the dying part didn't happen now though.

He backed up, hoping to reach the open door behind him before they finished kissing. This could still work as long as he could get out of here before they noticed him.

He was almost at the door when Persephone muttered, "Please, my Hell Beast. I'll let you suck on my toes if you put on the Lucifer costume."

"But you don't like it when I do that, honey-flower."

"But you like it, my sexy-wexy-lover-boy. And while you do that, I'll suck your c—"

"'Ew -ew." TMI even for a cupid. Tamuel skittered backwards, desperate to get out of the room before he saw something he'd never be able to forget. He turned ... and bounced off Hades' naked chest.

Damn you Fates. He'd obviously made enough noise to catch the God of the Underworld's attention. Rallying – and trying to ignore the God's raging hard-on that tented his jeans – he smiled up at Hades. "Happy All Hallows' Eve, Uncle."

Hades didn't smile. "I don't remember receiving notice from Eros that one of his cupids was coming down for a visit," he said smoothly, turning back to look at his wife. "Do you remember asking Eros to send one of his cupids down here, my passion flower?"

Persephone crossed her arms, shaking her head a little.

"No, I did not, pooky-wooky. What are you doing here, Tamuel?"

"Well, I—"

"I smell blood." Hades' gaze snapped to the blood dripping on the floor then at its source – the sigil carved into Tamuel's skin.

He made to back away, but Hades grabbed Tamuel by the wrist, lifting it to his nose. He sniffed at the bloody sigil then, black eyes flaring red as they met Tamuel's, he snarled, "You're corporeal. Who showed you that magic, boy?"

Shit. Shit. This so wasn't going how he'd planned – slip in, find Varagustus, get the information he wanted, steal a Hells-Key, travel to Tartarus and question Clodia, then back out before Hades even knew he'd come here. But there was no point lying to the angry God standing before him. Hiding his wince of pain as the God of the Underworld's fingers tightened around his wrist, he said, "Nobody, Uncle. I found it."

Hades growled, fingers tightening further – pain slashed through Tamuel as something snapped in his wrist. Hades' grip tightened as he barked out, "I don't believe you. Zeus and I made Persephone and Demeter rid the world of this heresy many centuries past." He leaned in closer, a growl in his throat, black eyes flashing orange then red. "Tell me who told you of this spell."

The God jerked his hand; something else snapped. Lights sparked before Tamuel's eyes and he almost went to his knees.

"Well?" Hades shook him.

Tears stinging his eyes, Tamuel managed to say, "I've always been ... interested in ... the Eleusinian Mysteries. I found ... writings on them."

"Impossible," Persephone said, coming to stand beside Hades. She might be pixie-like to her husband's towering brute, but in that moment, she was the far more frightening. "Who betrayed us?"

"I—" His mind whirled, trying to come up with something, anything, but the pain as Hades crushed his wrist made that impossible. Darkness whirled around him and he ...

Shaking brought him back to consciousness; pain spiked through him, the warmth of blood running down his arm – his suit was going to be ruined, he thought groggily. Someone was yelling something. More shaking and pain brought his attention back to the God still holding him up by his mangled wrist. "Wha?" he slurred.

"Tell us, cupid, or your body and your spirit won't leave the Underworld this All Hallows' Eve – or ever again."

Despite the danger and threat, Hades' beautiful voice coiled around Tamuel, drawing him in, making it impossible to deny him what he wanted, no matter how he'd promised not to tell on ... "Demeter."

"My mother?" Persephone said.

He nodded, then cried out again as Hades squeezed and broken bones ground together. Darkness threatened to take him down once more. "Please, my lord," he gasped. "My wrist. You're crushing ... it."

"Ease up, pumpkin pie. You don't want him to pass out before he tells you what we want to know."

"Whatever you say, honey bunny." He let go.

Tamuel dropped to the floor. He knew he shouldn't take his eyes off Hades, but couldn't help looking down at his shattered wrist. He almost fainted at the sight. But it wasn't so much the bones that poked through his skin that made him break into a cold sweat: the sigil was destroyed. He hadn't memorised it; had planned to copy it from one wrist to the other for his return but now …

"Oh Hades, look what you've done."

"It's no more than he deserves for using that spell."

Hades tapped his foot. Tamuel looked up at him, mind whirring, his thoughts clearer now that Hades had stopped inflicting pain. Eros had spent hours lecturing him when he was younger about the importance of dealing with what came next rather than what came after. He really wished he'd listened because if he didn't find some way of getting Hades and Persephone to understand, then there was no point in worrying if he could remember the sigil or not: he wasn't making it out of this room alive.

Trying to ignore the sick throbbing pain in his wrist and arm – and the fear he maybe had finally bitten off more than he could chew – he pushed to his feet, straightened his shoulders and met the God of the Underworld's angry gaze. He'd already broken his promise, so … "Demeter gave it into my keeping centuries ago."

"She wouldn't do that," Persephone said, delicate features filled with hurt and anger.

"She did."

"But we destroyed all the words together. Wiped all the followers' minds."

"Not all. She couldn't do that to her favourite priestess, Carianthe. She hid her from you and let her keep her memories. Carianthe wrote her life's work all over again in the last years of her life. After she died, Demeter couldn't bring herself to destroy it, so she gave it to me to hide with the other treasures I had in my keeping."

"Your mother," Hades snarled at Persephone. "I should have known she'd find some way of screwing this up. I just never thought she hated me so much that she'd risk this. Wait until I get my hands on her ... I'll—"

"You'll do nothing to my mother," Persephone said, grabbing her husband's hands as they made a wringing motion. "I will take her to task over this. But first, we must find out why Mum gave Tamuel a copy of the Eleusinian Mysteries Grimoire. Did she want you to use this spell?"

Hades turned to him, fire in his eyes. "Did she?" He grabbed Tamuel's wrist, pulling him up by it. "Did she?"

He clamped down on the scream, forcing himself to hold onto consciousness – he'd never seen his uncle this angry before. Didn't want to think what might happen if he passed out. "No," he ground out through clenched teeth, pain a writhing thing inside him. "She just wanted me ... to keep it safe ... in memory of her ... beloved priestess."

"Why did you look at it then?"

"Your mother said ... I might have use of ... certain spells one day ... when I was desperate. She said I was only to ... look at it then ... I would know when. Please, Uncle. My wrist."

Hades pulled him closer. "Did you tell anyone of it?"

"No!" Well, except for the ghost who had helped him realise what the spell was. But Hades didn't need to know about that. He met the God's angry gaze as he said earnestly, "I would never ... give this spell to anyone else. Never."

Hades stared him down for long moments, eyes sparking.

Hells, was he going to kill him? His uncle had always been kind to him. Much kinder than all the other Gods. Probably helped by the fact that Persephone had taken him under her wing for a while when he'd been a youth, allowing him to be trained alongside her Soteira at the

Amazonian and Gargarean warrior training camp; something no other cupid before or since had been allowed to do.

"Silly boy," Persephone tutted. "What did you think was going to happen when you were caught with this spell on your arm? You have to know it not only allows someone in and out of the Underworld in corporeal form, but allows a spirit to gain a body and use it to escape?"

"You weren't supposed ... to be here."

She shook her head at him. "My fondness for you may not be enough to get you out of trouble this time." She brushed her hand down the side of his face, frowning. "I really was hoping to get to my party on time this year."

He looked at her, desperately. "I had no choice. I made a vow."

"The Eternal Well accepted?"

"Yes," Tamuel grated.

She gasped, glancing at Hades before returning her attention to Tamuel. "This is what made you break one of our most sacred laws?"

"I need to speak to ... one of your guests," Tamuel panted, spots still sparking in front of his eyes. "I just need ... information ... to get my mother's power back."

A look flashed between Hades and Persephone before she said, "Enough, Hades. We need to hear what the boy has to say." The Goddess put her arm around Tamuel. "He doesn't deserve to be punished for what is obviously one of my mother's meddling visions."

"But that spell—"

"I'm sorry I ... used it ... I just ... want to get my mother's ... powers back to her. Without them, she'll only have ... a human life. I can't lose her ... or my father ... again. I just can't." He swallowed hard against pain of a different sort that thickened his throat. "Besides ... they deserve ... a true happy ever after. Like you have."

Hades shared a look with Persephone that made something in Tamuel's chest tighten, then suddenly let go his grip. Tamuel almost wept in relief as he clutched his broken arm to his chest, thankful Persephone was there to hold him up – despite her diminutive size, she was very strong.

"I wish I could help you with your parents' plight," Hades said quietly. "But I do not have your mother's powers, boy. Nor do I know where they are."

Tamuel took a few long, deep breaths, finally managing to push the pain aside as he'd been taught to do – at least enough for him to say steadily, "I know. But that witch-bitch Clodia does. And I know she's here. I know that you and Zeus tracked her down in the Void and imprisoned her in Tartarus for her hubris in stealing my mother's Goddess-given powers."

"I shoved her in a cell myself and set her punishment. But the power you say she stole is no longer in her."

He'd heard that too. "I want to ask her what happened to it," he said as Persephone began to shepherd him towards the couch.

"Given the fact she didn't tell me, no matter how much I tortured her, what makes you think she will tell you?"

"Because I have this." He pulled on the chain that hung around his neck, lifting it until the HeartsBlood Gem popped out from his shirt to swing in front of him. "Clodia tied her soul to this. With the right spell, I can compel her to answer my questions using the power the gem has over her."

Persephone lowered him to the couch. "This is the reason you decided to use that spell?"

"The only way to bring it here was if I was in corporeal

11

form. It's the only thing that will get Clodia to talk. But ... It won't work for me. I was hoping to speak to Varagustus first – the spell was supposed to take me to his cell."

"Varagustus?" Persephone shared another look with Hades. "Why Varagustus?"

"His knowledge of magical gems is greater than any before or after him. But I think he held a lot of knowledge back from his writings. I'm certain he will know what I need to do to use the gem."

Persephone looked up at her husband. "Hades ..."

"No good will come of it."

"It's what we've been waiting for," Persephone said, her hand on Hades' arm as she looked up into his eyes. "She's only gotten worse. She's not been anywhere for centuries. I had no idea when I agreed ..."

"Don't blame yourself for that, my blooming rose."

Persephone shook her head. "What matters blame if she's intrigued enough by this? Especially with the Hearts-Blood Gem in play. What if this is the true reason my mother sent him down here? She has always felt guilty about what happened. About the choices we all made. Please, honey-bee."

"But you know how our guest feels. I wouldn't want to force her, my spring's delight."

"It isn't your choice, bunny-wunny."

"Her who?" Tamuel asked.

They didn't answer, just had a staring match.

Finally, Hades threw his hands up, sighing gustily as he turned back to Tamuel. "Fine. Say I do agree to you travelling to Tartarus—"

"You will," Persephone said, beaming at him. He glared at her but she waved her hand at him as she took a seat next to Tamuel. "If for no other reason than you and your siblings do not wish that power to stay wherever it is. It unbalances things. It should be with the witch it was intended for – Tamuel's mother."

"So, you'll help me?" He couldn't believe his luck in this turnaround. He had no idea giving up Demeter would lead to this – he'd deal with her anger later. Right now, he wasn't going to look a gift horse in the mouth. Not even what could be a Trojan one.

Hades nodded begrudgingly. "I will. But there are three issues. The first being, I will not let you anywhere in my kingdom with that spell etched on your arm for anyone to see. Persephone can heal your wrist, but that sigil will not be left intact. You will need to remember it, only carving its mirror into your other wrist just before you wish to travel back."

Tamuel swallowed hard. "Not a problem." He hoped. He just needed a moment to sit down and go into his memory vault and retrieve it.

Hades nodded. "The second is the matter of the ticking clock. If you don't mirror that spell work and get back through the portal by the time the clock strikes twelve in the Earthly Realm on All Hallows' Eve, your soul *will* be cursed to stay trapped down here forever."

He opened his mouth to say it wouldn't be a problem, but Persephone raised her hand, her voice echoing strangely as she said, "The veil is thinning and time is constantly changing. This year more than any others. The current alignment of the stars heralds dark portents that place a shadow over all the Realms." She blinked and swallowed hard. "It is not a good time to travel through the Underworld, especially for a corporeal being."

He didn't like the sound of that. Not that it mattered – it was now or never. "Lucky I'm wearing this then." He gestured to the chronometer. If it worked as it should, it would tell him how the time shifted and warn him of changes in relation to the Earthly Realm – no matter what the stars heralded with their eerie portents. "I should be out of here well in time, even if the weeks I currently have turn to days. As long as I can have a Hells-Key?"

Hades' brow lowered. Persephone coughed. They glared at each other, making Tamuel wish he could read minds because he was certain there was quite the conversation going on.

Finally, Hades rolled his eyes. "I will give you a Hells-Key to move around the Underworld with more ease. But there is one last sticking point, one I have no say over."

"And what is that?"

"Varagustus didn't write those treatises on gems. The woman who did is not one of my prisoners."

"What? But if I can't find out how to use the gem, then my trip here is pointless."

Hades raised his hand. "She is not a prisoner. She is a valued member of my household. And she has refused to see anyone for centuries – aside from us, the servants and those she wants to interview of course."

"I will do whatever it takes to make her agree to help me."

"She may want the HeartsBlood Gem in payment," Persephone said.

He glanced down at the gem hanging around his neck. It wasn't his to give but ... "Fine. I cannot go home empty-handed."

Hades and Persephone shared a look again before she said, "Then I will take you to her. But first, I will heal your arm – Korinna doesn't like the sight of blood."

"Korinna?" His mouth dried. "You don't mean Korinna Soteira?"

"The very one." Persephone shot him a brief, sad smile as she began the healing.

Korinna Soteira. The name rang in his head, his thoughts too lost to the past to truly feel the pain of the healing as it burned through his skin and bones.

Korinna had not only broken his heart but had crushed it under her dainty foot almost two thousand years ago. The rejection had left him bleeding and wishing for death.

But none of that mattered now. All that mattered was his vow. "Take me to her. I'm sure she will speak to me."

She owed him that at least.

CHAPTER
TWO

Korinna stared at the screen before her, the words hazing. She pressed her fingers against the bridge of her nose, squeezing her eyes shut. Tired. She was just tired. If her Aunty Seph was here rather than on earth celebrating spring with her mother and sisters, she'd insist that she eat and rest.

But how could she when she still hadn't saved those who had been under her care – even if the only way to save them now was to find their lost souls and send them to Elysium?

All those people. Their screams. Their cries for help as the volcano dust choked them, encasing them where they stood, still rang in her mind. Men, women, children. The entire beautiful city of Pompeii. All dead.

Her fault. All her fault.

If anyone needed to pay for their sins, it was her.

She only wished Seph would stop trying to make her feel better. How was a person supposed to get over something like that? Hades was far more understanding of the need driving her. She couldn't feel better. Wouldn't feel better. She deserved to live in darkness for eternity.

Countless centuries of research and study and she'd come up with nothing ... until now.

The Eleusinian Mysteries. She was certain the key she needed was held in the ancient grimoire. It was thought destroyed, but she knew differently. The last lost soul she'd interviewed in their Underworld cell had told her what Demeter had done. Now she just had to figure out some way of asking Demeter to give the grimoire to her without Seph or Hades finding out. Not so easy when Demeter never came down here, hating Hades as she did. And it wasn't like she could go to Demeter – she was bound to this place by her vow; an unfortunate wording issue making her unable to travel. And of course, she couldn't use her magic to help send a message. And she couldn't send a message via one of the other Soteira – they might be her friends and sisters, but their loyalties lay with Seph.

She rubbed her eyes again. The problem was, she wasn't devious enough. A dreadful fault for someone who lived among the Gods, whose deviousness was legend. The only time in her life that she'd ever got away with anything was with Tam—

She brutally cut the thought off before it could truly form and concentrated on the screen in front of her again.

She didn't need him or anyone else to help her figure out how to do this. Seph was forever saying Korinna was one of the smartest people she'd ever known. Those smarts had led her to discovering how to save the souls she'd sent spiralling into the Void and convey them to Elysium where they would live in peace and happiness forever more; to knowledge of the spell that would allow her to do it.

All that was standing between her and it was her ability to contact Demeter *and* get the Goddess to give her the grimoire without tipping off Hades or Seph. They'd destroy the ancient book of spells before she could use it if they so much as got whisper of its existence. She couldn't allow that to happen.

She rubbed her temples, eyes closed, but nothing came to her.

Perhaps she should take a walk, clear her head.

She stood, made it half-way across the room before dizziness hit. The room swayed around her. She staggered to the couch Seph had placed in front of the fireplace when she'd last decorated Korinna's room and fell into it. How long had she been staring at the computer screen?

Her stomach chose that moment to growl.

Oh. When was the last time she'd eaten?

She couldn't remember. Food was brought for her and placed at her elbow every day, morning, noon and night, but if she was deep in her work, she often forgot it was there. They would take away her untouched tray and replace it with another, so it was impossible to tell when she'd last eaten by looking at the tray currently on her desk – a plate of her favourite lasagne, now cold, the cheese congealed on top with no obvious signs she'd touched it.

Way too long, going by how dizzy and weak she was. Damn it. How stupid could she be? It would do no one any good if she passed out. She sniffed, catching a whiff of herself for the first time. She couldn't remember the last time she'd showered and changed either. She raked her hand through her hair, fingers getting caught in the knots she'd ignored when she'd piled the mass of greasy curls on top of her head this morning. Or was it yesterday morning?

Damn it. Hades would give her a lecture if he found her

in this condition. And then tell Seph. And Seph would worry.

She wasn't sure why he hadn't come in already. He wasn't as much of a worry-wart as Aunty Seph – only checking on her a few times a week – but he would normally have been in by now. She glanced at the large chronometer – her own design – on her wall. Its hands showed her the shifting of time due to the thinning of the veil. All Hallows' Eve. Of course.

Seph's Halloween party. It explained why he'd been such a grump the last time he'd come in to check on her. She'd thought it was because it was the time of year designated for Seph to be in the Upper Realms. Hades was always a grump for the months – years down here – that his wife was away from him thanks to the bargain between him and his mother-in-law that Seph would be with her in the Northern and Southern Hemisphere Springs. It was why Seph had always made such a thing out of celebrating Halloween – it allowed them to see each other in this time of separation with the veil thinning as it did. Although Hades had never liked having to dress up in whatever couples-inspired outfit Seph decided upon in any given year.

Thank the Gods Seph had given up requesting Korinna's presence at those events many centuries ago. It was one guilt trip she certainly hadn't needed.

So, shower or food first? The room still swayed around her when she stood, giving her the answer. She pushed away from the couch, heading to her desk and the cold lasagne. Dizziness surged. She staggered, tripped over the rug, hurtling across the floor, arms wheeling.

"Rinna," a voice called out. Then hands caught her,

steadying her. She looked up into achingly familiar indigo eyes.

"Tam."

He smiled at her. Actually smiled at her. "I'm here. Are you okay?"

She tore herself from his grasp, all signs of dizziness gone as fury overwhelmed her. With a growl, she punched him square in the mouth.

Tamuel staggered back, touched his bleeding lip, eyes wide. "What the Hella, Rinna? What was that for?"

"As if you don't know."

"I don't."

She hit him again.

The look on his face was comical as he staggered again. She would have laughed except she was too mad.

Mad? No, that didn't express what she was. She was furious. Betrayed. Hurt.

He'd promised to stay by her side and help her with her first assignment – to keep Vesuvius asleep and ensure the people of Pompeii remained safe. He had known how nervous she'd been; how much she'd doubted her ability to take on her dead mother's post and do it justice.

Then he'd left without a word the day before she was due to leave.

After all they'd shared, he'd treated her as if she was nothing.

And she'd never forgiven him.

She'd spent months looking for him, waiting to hear something, anything, every day of silence increasing her anger, her despair, her hurt. Enough that she missed the signs a true Guardian wouldn't have missed. Enough that she had acted erroneously and made everything so much worse.

His fault for leaving. His fault for not being there to help her see what she missed. And worse, his fault for not being there in the weeks and months after to help her, with the balancing warmth of his powers and his friendship, to help her cope with what had happened. She'd failed as Guardian of Pompeii. She'd needed her best friend, had cried out for him. After promising her he would always come when she needed him, there had only been silence and grief and an endless loneliness that had never abated.

If not for him – for his lies, for his leaving, for all his betrayals – she would never have tried the impossible; would never have been forced into making a vow that, one way or another, would bring her death.

She'd long wanted to make him pay, but he was beyond her reach, in Eros' service. Sharing his love around like a typical cupid no doubt – why she'd ever thought he'd be any different she didn't know. Their friendship – it had all been in her head. He'd obviously never felt the same, no matter that he'd made her think he did, because he'd left without a word, hadn't replied to any of her letters, had ignored her entirely. Everything they'd shared was a lie.

She punched him again, not caring how much her knuckles hurt now.

"Oh dear," Hades drawled as he caught Tamuel and set him back on his feet. "I don't think she's going to help you like you thought she would."

"Korinna dear. Are you okay?"

Hades had a shit-eating grin on his face, Seph a frown of concern on hers. "I'm fine," she snapped, wanting them all to just go away and take the betraying arsehole with them.

"Is *she* okay?" Tam asked, touching his split lip. "What

21

LEISL LEIGHTON

about me? I'm the one whose been sucker-punched for no good reason."

She glared at him. "No good reason?" She lifted her fist, ignoring the throb in her knuckles – it had been a long time since she'd sparred and her body wasn't used to the pain.

He raised his hand in self-defence. "Whatever I did, I'm sorry."

"Whatever you did? Whatever you did!" Hells, she sounded like a shrieking banshee. Nobody had ever made her lose her cool like he could. How was it that he could still do it all these centuries later? "You left. Without a word. After you promised to stay. When you knew I needed you the most!"

"Hang on. That wasn't my fault. Eros just came and took me. Besides, you never really needed me. I got that message loud and clear when you ignored the letters I sent to you. I might not have been able to come with you like I promised, but *you* were the one who abandoned our friendship."

She jerked. "I never abandoned ... I never got any ..." She snapped her mouth closed, blew out a loud breath then, pointing her finger at him, said, "Don't turn this around on me. I never got any letters from you, liar. And you ignored my letters!"

"What?" He looked insulted – and hurt. "But that's not possible. I wrote every day, then when you didn't reply, once a week. I thought maybe you were just busy with your duties. I begged Eros to let me go to you – but it took months of bargaining every privilege I had to make him agree. As soon as he did, I went looking for you but Pompeii was gone. I went to the training camp but you weren't there and nobody would tell me what had happened or where you had gone. It was like you'd disappeared off the face of

22

the earth. I thought maybe you'd died." He glanced around him, his face paling. "You're not dead, are you?"

She snorted, not believing a word of what he'd just said. "No. Did my fist in your face feel incorporeal to you?"

He rubbed his chin. "Then why are you here? *How* are you here?"

"I'm a Soteira. Hades allows us to reside here with Persephone as her handmaidens."

"Right. But that doesn't answer why I couldn't find you or why you abandoned your post."

"I don't owe you an explanation." Her gaze bore into him as she tried to let fury burn away the hurt his words caused.

"Surely you've not been here since I left?"

She pressed her lips against all the words she wanted to shout at him and just said. "Pretty much."

"But what about your plans? You wanted to travel the world after your contracted years as Guardian of Pompeii were up. To keep helping people."

She shrugged. "Plans change."

"Not this much."

She glanced at Hades and Seph. They watched her carefully, as they always did, as she wished they wouldn't. She wasn't breakable – you couldn't break what was already broken. But they obviously hadn't told him anything. Good. Not that she thought they would. They'd kept her secrets all these years. They were hardly about to spill them to one too-handsome auburn-haired cupid.

"Rinna, what happened?" he asked more softly.

She hated that his voice could still get inside her like that; curling around her heart, making her want to soften, to confide. She straightened her back. "I decided research was my forte. And Hades has been kind enough to let me live in his palace where I can do my research undisturbed." She turned back, glowering at him. "So, if you don't mind, I would like to get back to what I was doing before you interrupted."

"I ..." His fingers grazed her arm before she could turn away. "Rinna, please. You have to believe me. I did send you letters. I did try to find you."

"I don't believe you." She bit back on the sob in her voice, too aware of the others watching.

"I wasn't allowed to leave Eros' side for an entire year. I was bound to him. I couldn't break free until I had permission."

"And it took *you* a whole year to get permission?"

Tam lifted his hands and let them drop. "Eros was intractable. A fact you would have known if you had got my letters."

"Well, I didn't get any letters."

His gaze raked over her face. "And I didn't get any from you, yet you say you sent them."

"I did. Are you saying somebody kept them from us? Why would they do that?"

"I have no idea. But the real question is, why won't you believe me? Why would you think I would leave without a word? You obviously think very little of me."

"I ..." She clenched her fists at her side, trying to stop the tremors shaking through her body from showing. "You. Left. Me."

Tam took a step closer, his violet eyes ablaze with indignation that seemed so real. "Not. By. Choice!"

He stood so close now, his breath brushed over her face. She stepped closer. "So. You. Say."

His jaw clenched. "It seems to me like you were just

annoyed that I didn't deign to get your permission before I left."

"Deign to get my permission?" Her fingers curled into fists.

"Oh-oh. That was a mistake," Hades said, snickering.

"Hades, you need to do something," Persephone whispered.

"Why? This is fun," Hades whispered back.

She ignored them, attention boring into the annoying cupid in front of her. "Deign. To. Get. My. Permission?" She poked him in the chest with each word, her finger bouncing off firm, defined muscle.

He grabbed her finger, holding it firmly in his warm grasp. Fire zapped through her veins at the contact. Ah Hells. He'd always been cute, but now ... He'd grown into his demi-God-hood in the almost two thousand years since she'd seen him. And how! She took a gulping breath and forced herself to stare unblinking into his beautiful eyes. "How can you say that to me? After all we shared?"

His full mouth thinned as her question struck him. Then, jaw clenched, eyes blazing, he asked, "How is that different from you accusing me of betrayal after all we shared?"

"I ... I ... Get out." She tore her hand from his and pointed at the door, her powers fizzing inside her, sparking on her fingertips. She mercilessly pushed them back. She couldn't trust them. Not after ... "Get out before I do something I can't take back."

"My pleasure, my Queen." Tam bowed, waving his hand, an obvious mocking of the gesture he used to make to her; one that had always made her laugh. It should have made her angrier, but the anger died the moment she saw the mark on his wrist.

Gasping, she grasped a hold of his arm. "What is this?" The marking, marred by an obvious attempt to heal it, was damaged by a nasty scar running through its middle but it was unmistakably from the lost Eleusinian Mysteries Grimoire. Every reference she'd managed to get her hands on had spoken about the unmistakable difference in the spell work and sigils – and this was different. Even damaged, it made her skin both crawl and shiver in excitement. "This spell. Where did you get it?"

"Persephone! I thought you'd healed him," Hades said, moving as if to stand between them.

"I did," she answered, appearing at Hades side, reaching for Tam's hand. "But I can't make a spell like that disappear. It's damaged though. Nobody will be able to copy and use it." She turned her gaze on Korinna. "What I want to know is how my darling Soteira knows what it is."

Korinna's heart pounded faster as she glanced between her mentor and Hades, their expressions harder than she'd ever seen, and aimed at her. "It's the answer," she whispered. "Not this spell particularly, but where it comes from."

A light of understanding lit Persephone's eyes. "You should have come to me. Told me you were looking for the grimoire."

"Why? You wouldn't have been able to help. You and Demeter never took any notice of what your worshippers did until they created their spells, until a grieving lover created and used this one." She gestured at Tamuel's wrist. "Then you destroyed everything they'd created, just so nobody could use any death or soul translocation spells again. Not only could you not tell me what I needed to know, I knew you would never let me have it."

Seph drew closer, touched her cheek. "My darling girl.

Of course I would. If it is what you need to help get over your self-imposed exile and stop grieving, I would have searched the Realms to find someone who remembered it."

She blinked rapidly. Of course, Seph had no idea what the consequences would be if she used the grimoire ... but she couldn't let herself think of that guilt and grief now. Not when the answers were so close to being in her grasp. She looked back at Tam. "This is how you got here in corporeal form?"

He nodded.

She wanted to demand why he would do such a risky thing, but too many other questions vied for attention and came spilling out. "But how do you come to have that spell? Did you find someone who remembered it? Do you only have this spell? Do you know the location of the Eleusinian Mysteries Grimoire?"

"Not just the location. I have the entire grimoire," he said.

Excitement fluttered in her chest. "You've got a copy of the entire grimoire?"

"I do." He smiled. A smile she used to love; a smile that had encouraged her into one mischievous scheme after another, overriding her more cautious nature; a smile that had got her through so much; a smile she had missed like no other when it was gone from her life.

But she didn't have time for such things now, so steeling herself against it, she said through a tight jaw, "You're not lying?"

"I would never lie to you, Rinna. Not about the letters I sent or trying to find you. And certainly not about this."

Her breath a shallow pant as she looked deep in his eyes – he'd never been able to lie to her. At least, she hadn't thought he could until he'd left and she'd realised she'd been fooled. But what she saw in his eyes now, openness and a need for her trust, it made her nod. Even though she still didn't quite believe him about the rest, she believed him about this. She held out her hand. "Then show me."

He snorted. "I don't have it on me. Do you think I would carry such a thing around, especially down here?"

"Of course not."

"But I am happy to give it to you after I'm finished here."

Korinna trembled, her breath a rough gasp in her throat. "You will give it to me?" The very thing she'd been looking for to right her past wrongs? It seemed too good to be true. "Why would you do that? It's priceless."

He flicked his hand. "Its only value to me was in getting me to and from this place in corporeal form. But now, its value is far beyond anything I had thought it."

"How is that?"

"Because I will give it to you only after you help me."

CHAPTER
THREE

The wonder in Korinna's eyes evaporated, to be replaced by bitterness. Tamuel swore deep inside. He hated seeing that bitterness in his best friend's eyes – ex-best friend according to her. Her fury was more welcome than the rancour and disappointment currently dulling the golden-topaz of her large eyes.

"You wish to hold my services to ransom?"

The way she said it – it cut him to the core. That she would think so little of him ... but then again, she already had thought so little of him given she believed he'd left without a word; without trying to find her. And he'd thought so little of her for the same reason.

Someone had got between them, of that he was certain, even if he had no idea why. But now wasn't the time to get into that. Now he had to make her agree to help him – the rest could wait. He gentled his smile. "No, of course not. But I cannot give you the grimoire until I return to the surface to retrieve it, and I cannot do that until I have finished my quest here."

"Quest?"

"To find and retrieve my mother's powers, stolen from her by the ancient Vestal High Priestess, Clodia."

Her gaze flickered in interest and she turned an accusing gaze on Hades and Persephone. "Clodia is here? Why didn't you tell me?"

The Goddess of Spring waved a hand at the desk. "You have been rather busy with your research, dear. I'm certain nobody wanted to disturb you with such insignificant news."

"Insignificant news? The fact that Hades has finally captured the outlaw Vestal High Priestess who tried to steal Goddess-given power – and who was last seen with the HeartsBlood Gem – isn't insignificant news?" She spun around, pacing to her desk as she mumbled, "It's like you don't know me at all."

"I don't know why you're getting upset about it now, especially given our little cupid here has the HeartsBlood Gem with him."

"What?" She spun around to face him, her hand out as if to reach for the gem. "Why didn't you start with that? How did you get it? Let me see."

Tamuel couldn't help chuckling in appreciation of the fire of interest in her eyes. It reminded him so much of the past when she'd become fascinated by some topic and wouldn't let up until she knew everything. "To answer your questions, a) I was getting to telling you about it, but you punched me; b) my mother gave it to me after she took it from Clodia in our showdown with her on Valentine's Eve; and c) here it is." Slowly, he pulled the gem out from where he wore it under his shirt.

The red glow of it reflected in her eyes as she drew near. "It's beautiful." She reached for it, stumbled.

He dropped the gem, the weight of it banging against

his chest, and caught her. She trembled, but he didn't think it had anything to do with excitement. She was almost skin and bone. He'd not noticed it when they'd walked in and she'd punched him. But now he had his hands on her shoulders, steadying her, he couldn't help but feel how fragile she was. Or notice how the mass of her curly black hair – that she'd always kept scrupulously clean even though she always raked it into a tight ponytail or bun – was matted and oily. Or that the lemon and spice scent of her he'd always loved was overtaken with the distinct pungency of someone who'd not had a shower in days, possibly longer.

What had she been doing to herself? And why the Hella had Hades and Persephone let her get like this? Was she being punished?

In a blaze of anger, he turned to them, but stilled as her hand landed on his chest, fingers flexing.

Fire zapped over him, through him, almost as if she'd used her power on him. But she hadn't.

Her gaze flew to his, eyes flaring with awareness. Of him? That seemed impossible. While he'd loved her with a passion that went well beyond friendship when they'd trained together, she had never shown any romantic inter-est. Their friendship had been close – the closest he'd ever had – but nothing more than that. Not that he'd had expec-tation for more – the curse placed on him by Eros at his birth made certain of that. The curse had been the only way Eros had of saving him from Clodia; the only way he could take him as one of his own, given Tamuel's father was only a demi-God and his mother a human witch – not the ideal combination for a cupid; the only way he could stop him from giving into the human weakness of falling in love. A cupid couldn't get tangled in his customers' needs and desires. He had to stay separate if he was to help lead the lovers in the direction the Fates desired for them.

Love was for others, not for them.

So, he'd bound Tamuel to him in the only way he could, cursing him to find love for others but never for himself. He had woven a cryptic 'out' clause into the curse, but nobody had ever been able to figure out the bit about the broken mirror, equal and opposite. It made no sense – but that was Eros for you. And the God wouldn't talk about it; he said Tamuel would need to work it out for himself. That was how curses worked.

That was all very well for Eros to say, but it was particularly painful when the way this curse worked didn't stop him from falling in love – a fact he'd discovered when he'd met Rinna, fallen in love with her, but could never act on it. He could never declare his love while the curse made certain nobody would ever fall in love with him. And given he couldn't make sense out of the cryptic mirror crap in the curse, he was doomed.

Except … Rinna's eyes were lit with something he'd never expected to see there: passion. Desire.

Although, those emotions, while often tied to love, didn't mean there was love. Perhaps …

No, he was wrong. He was just projecting what he wanted to see – because the truth was, he still loved her as much as he ever had. He'd thought he'd hardened himself enough to no longer feel it, but he'd been wrong.

Even as she'd punched him, he knew he'd been wrong. And now, her fingers flexing against him while she looked up at him like that … it was doing things to him he didn't want. Certainly not here, under Hades' and Persephone's eagle eyes.

He quickly set Rinna away from him, letting go of her as

soon as he knew she was steady, the gem swinging against his chest.

Her gaze finally broke from his and went to the stone. She reached for it.

He stepped back, holding the gem out of reach. "Ah-ah. Not yet."

Aggravation flickered over her lovely but too-thin features – her chin and cheekbones more pointed, her eyes larger in her heart-shaped face. Her gaze went from the stone to him. "Don't be a tease. Let me see it."

"I will, but ..." He raised a finger. "Only after you have eaten and showered."

"You sound like Seph and Hades."

"And you sound grumpy. Like you do when you need to sleep."

"I don't need to sleep."

She wavered on her feet.

He turned to Hades and Persephone. "Why is she being tortured like this?"

Persephone's perfectly manicured brows shot up. "Tortured? She is beloved, not tortured."

"She's not being tortured," Hades boomed at the same time. "What makes you think I would do that to someone as beloved to my wife as Korinna? She is looked after as an honoured guest."

"Really?" Tamuel asked, gesturing at Rinna. "Then why is she skin and bone and wavering on her feet as if she hasn't had a proper meal or a good sleep for weeks?"

Persephone's eyes widened as she took a good look at her favourite Soteira and then turned to hit Hades in the chest. "You promised you wouldn't let her get like she did last time she got lost in her research. How could you have let her do this to herself again?"

Hades stepped away from his wife, rubbing his chest. "I didn't. I made certain she had three meals a day and came in every few days to make certain she showered and slept."

"Did she eat the meals? Did you stay to make certain she actually got in the shower? That she actually climbed into bed and went to sleep?"

Hades looked sheepish. "I didn't think to check."

"Hello? I'm standing right here." Rinna waved at them, her motions jerky – possibly due to annoyance, but Tamuel thought it was more likely due to exhaustion and under-nourishment. "Stop talking about me as if I'm a baby unable to care for myself."

"Well," Persephone said, hands on her hips as she glared at her protégé. "If you managed to actually look after yourself without supervision, I would. How could you have let yourself get like this again? Hades wasn't the only one who gave me promises."

Rinna's gaze dipped. "I didn't exactly break my promise. I ate and showered ... sometimes."

"And when was the last time you slept?" Persephone guided Rinna to the lounge in front of the fire – this one carved out of the black rock like the one in Hades' lounge room, but rather than a jagged bite, its mantel was carved with depictions of spring – obviously Persephone's work, as were the tapestries on the walls and the colours of spring within the rugs and furnishings.

Rinna rubbed her brow as she sat. "Umm, a week ago?" Persephone angled her a look. "Maybe more," she admitted softly.

"Hmm. That is hardly keeping your promise."

"I did better than last time. I did remember to eat. And shower."

"Not enough. Tamuel is right, you are skin and bone and ready to collapse."

"I was going to eat but then you came in with Tam." She gestured at the unappealing lump of lasagne on the desk.

Persephone gave her a withering look. "You can't eat that now. Hades, please call for more food and ask Dianna to prepare a lovely hot bath for our girl – she needs a good soak. And some relaxing herbs in the water to help her sleep."

"Don't fuss. You've got a party to get to. I don't want you to be late."

Ignoring Rinna, Hades waved his hand and disappeared in a whirl of black and fire-red smoke.

Rinna moved forward on the couch as if she was about to stand, but Persephone's grip on her tightened. "Where are you off to?"

"Umm, to have a bath?"

"And?"

"To eat?"

"And?"

Rinna glared at her mentor for a long moment. "Oh, don't be like that, Seph. I don't need to sleep. Not now." Her gaze went to Tamuel and the gem lying against his chest. "There's too much to do. Besides, Tamuel still hasn't told me why he needs my help. And given the spell he's used and the fact he's using what looks like my chronometer design—"

"You created this?" he asked, looking down at the steam-punk looking watch on his wrist. He'd had no idea she was the creator of the book of magical contraptions he loved to potter with.

She waved her hand as if it was nothing. "It was a

phase. Given you're wearing the chronometer, I gather you have a time restriction."

"I do. This spell could only be cast at the end of sunset on All Hallows' Eve and lasts until midnight. It was just before eight o'clock in the Earthly Realm when I cast it and crossed through the portal. By the chronometer's calculations when I landed here, four hours Earthly Realm time gives me at least a month down here—"

"Only if the thinning of the veil doesn't make our time closer to Earthly Realm time."

"Don't forget what—"

He shot a warning glance at Persephone as she went to blurt out the worrisome information she'd dropped on them earlier about this All Hallows' Eve Realm-alignment being even trickier than usual. He didn't want Rinna to worry – she needed to rest. "I won't forget."

"Forget what?" Rinna asked, gazing suspiciously between them.

"To set the alarm. You don't have to keep reminding me, Persephone. I'm no longer a child. I am capable of looking after myself."

She snorted. "Your actions today would seem to indicate otherwise."

"I think it's turned out all right." Tamuel shot her cheeky smile, thankfully making her chuckle. "Don't worry. I don't plan to get stuck here. I won't be able to help my mother if I do. But even with the trickiness of the spell and everything ..." He turned to Rinna. "There's still plenty of time for you to rest before helping me."

"Tamuel is right." Persephone said, smiling beneficently at him before returning her attention to her Soteira. "So, no arguing. And no more punishing yourself for something that was truly not your fault."

Rinna's gaze shadowed just before she turned away so he could no longer see her expression. But he could tell something wasn't right – she held her shoulders so stiffly it looked like her spine would snap with the effort. "I ... umm ... I'm not punishing myself."

Persephone grasped Rinna's hands, held them even when it looked like her Soteira wanted to pull away. "Remember who you are lying to, my darling one," she said softly, brushing another stray lock of hair behind Rinna's ear. "It is time it stopped." She glanced over at Tamuel. "Maybe my mother knows what she is about. Maybe now is the right time to forgive yourself."

CHAPTER
FOUR

"Forgive myself? I can never do that," Rinna whispered harshly. "Never."

She glanced at him briefly, and for the first time since he'd walked in, the first time since he'd known her, Tamuel saw something he'd never thought to see in her: vulnerability. And a hurt so deep, it ached inside him.

What had happened to make her like this?

Did it have something to do with what happened to Pompeii? Nobody had ever been able to tell him exactly what had occurred, let alone why she'd left her post, but he'd never believed the disaster had been her fault. Ultimately, if the Fates had decided Pompeii was to end like it had, then it would happen. No amount of magic could stop a fixed point of destiny from occurring. Surely, she knew that. Didn't she?

Looking at her, at how broken she seemed by whatever Persephone referred to, by the very fact she'd hidden here in Hades' Palace for two thousand years by the sound of things, he couldn't help thinking perhaps she didn't.

For a perfectionist like Korinna Soteira, what happened

to Pompeii would have been the ultimate in failure. Especially after she'd dreamed for years of taking up her dead mother's post and doing her proud.

Why had he never thought of this before? Perhaps she was right about him. He *was* a shit friend.

He stepped forward, wanting to add his words to Persephone's, to try to make Rinna see what the rest of them did, but a servant — a Soteira like Rinna — appeared next to Persephone. "The bath is ready," she said. "And cook says the food will be sent up in ten minutes or so."

"Is Lord Hades getting into his costume yet, Dianna?" Persephone asked.

Dianna grimaced. "I saw him throwing it in the fire, my Lady."

"Aggravating man. I better go deal with him while you take care of Korinna."

"I can take care of myself," Rinna said grumpily.

Persephone just patted her hand. "Please, let Dianna take care of you. For me."

Rinna glowered at her mentor and grumbled, "Fine." She glanced at Tamuel, the look on her face questioning.

"I'll go eat too. I'll come back later."

She nodded briskly and disappeared into her bedroom with Dianna, leaving Tamuel to follow Persephone out the carved ebony door.

As it closed behind him, he asked, "What happened to her? Why is she down here? Why did you say she was punishing herself? It's not because she thinks what happened is her fault, right? You wouldn't let her think that, would you?"

She stopped his barrage of questions by holding up her hand. "You, better than anyone, should know things are never that simple."

"What happened? I have to know."

Persephone glanced back at the door, biting her lip for a moment before turning back to him. "That is not my story to tell, young cupid. But if you play your cards right, you might just get her to tell you herself."

"Play my cards right?"

She touched his cheek, the gesture as intimate as ones he'd received from his mother, Jules, since they'd found each other. "There is a loophole to every curse, my dear boy. I think Korinna is the one to help you find it. Now," she clapped her hands together and stepped back before he could do more than gape at her. "Go eat. There'll be something set up in the dining hall for you. Then once you've had your meal, you can come back and settle into your room and get some rest. I instructed Dianna to give Korinna one of Hypnos' sleeping potions, so she should sleep for hours."

"Are you heading off to your party?"

"Yes — after I've got my costume-hating husband in hand. We won't be back until after your deadline has passed — I hope not to see you down here then. I trust you to look after our girl."

"Of course," Tamuel said. Although he doubted very much she'd let him. He touched his aching jaw — the warrior-witch still had a mean right hook.

"Good." She touched his shoulder. "I hope I'm correct and you're the exact man for the job. And don't forget what I said about the portents. Don't expect things to go to plan."

"I never do," he said, tapping the chronometer. "I wasn't joking about the alarm. It will tell me the moment anything changes."

"Very well. Good luck, my dearest boy." She spun

around and disappeared from his sight, a brush of warm, flower-scented air the only sign she'd been there.

Tamuel stared at the carvings of flora and fauna on the door, his mind a-whirl.

He'd not expected any of this when he'd set out on his quest, and while he wanted to help Rinna, he couldn't forget what had brought him here.

He had to get his mother's powers back. Without them, she would eventually die a human death. And when she did, her soulmate, his father, would find some way to follow her into death and be with her in Elysium. And then Tamuel would be all alone. Again.

He'd sacrificed so much to break the curse that had destroyed his family and bring his parents back together, bring them *all* back together, as a family. And he'd succeeded. They were together, but only for one human lifetime. It wasn't enough. Not nearly enough. He couldn't lose them again.

It was why he'd made his vow to the Eternal Well, tying his lifeforce into his promise: do or die. He couldn't allow their love to be destroyed by something as simple as death. Nothing would stop him. Certainly not the fact that being with Korinna Soteira was going to hurt.

He knew she would never love him, but he never imagined she would hate him.

At least he could change that. He had to make her believe he *had* been devastated when Eros took him from the camp in the Ceraunian Mountains where they'd been trained by Amazonian and Gargarean warriors, witches and warlocks. If only he could share his memories with her of that time, then maybe she would believe him. Because if he knew one thing about his friend it was this: she would never let him help her if she didn't trust him.

He paused in his pacing. Perhaps he could let her see his memories. There was something he'd read in one of the Stevens' grimoires that touched on memory sharing. He could find a quiet spot and enter the trance to retrieve the exact wording of the spell from his memory vault. Although he really needed to use the energy required for that kind of trance-work to extract the precise design for the sigil from there first. And it would take days, possibly weeks, to power up enough to extract both memories to the degree he would need to succeed with either of those tasks. And he'd have to be very careful not to tap into the tenuous link between him and the magical ark or power he'd used to get here – the link to that power secured his way home. He would need all the power there to get back to the Earthly Realm in his current form.

He sighed. Any other time this wouldn't be so difficult, but down here in the Underworld, with the power fluctuations that were bound to occur due to the Realms realigning, not to mention the death magic all around that was a constant drag on his cupid power, making him rely more on his warlock power, nothing was going to be easy.

So, prioritise. To get out of here, he needed that sigil. Helping Rinna could happen after. *Would* happen after.

However, none of that could happen until he'd refuelled. Opening that portal and stepping through had taken a lot more out of him than he'd bargained on even with using the power stored in the ark. Probably not helped by the pain of having his arm pulverised and then his face used as a punching bag. He touched his chin and winced. He wished he'd asked Persephone to heal his bruises and split lip before she went. It was times like this he wished he'd got more of a share of his father's powers – Bastien had healed all of them after the fight with

Clodia without breaking a sweat. At least being a cupid meant he'd heal faster than most others would. He should be perfectly fine in twelve hours or so. It was going to be fun eating until then. Maybe he'd ask for soup.

Sighing, he headed down the hall to the dining room.

An hour later when he returned to Rinna's rooms, he was shushed by Dianna, who was just coming out of the bedroom. "She's sound asleep," she whispered.

"Did she eat?"

She nodded. "And had a much-needed shower – I couldn't talk her into the bath." She walked closer, her chin lowering so she looked up at him through her lashes in a sultry move that would normally have had his hormones sitting up and taking notice – but not a twitch.

"Hades created a room on the other side of her quarters," she continued, her every move seductive – she was a handmaiden of a fertility Goddess after all. She gestured at the door in the curved wall to the left of the entryway, her wheat-coloured hair swishing against the upper curve of her bottom. "The Lady Persephone wanted you to be close by in case Korinna needs you. She sometimes has … nightmares."

"I'll keep an ear out."

She bit her lip as her gaze raked over him. "I've put some more appropriate clothing for you to wear in the wardrobe and made up your bed." He glanced down at his crumpled suit, blood spattering his pant leg.

"If you need anything," she said, touching Tamuel's chest with a blood-red fingernail. "Just ring this bell." She snapped her fingers and a bell appeared in her hand.

Tamuel edged a step back. In the past he would have happily taken up her not-so-subtle offer, but now that he'd seen Rinna again ... "Aren't you expected at Lady Perse-phone's party?"

Dianna smiled slowly. "I have time. I'm not part of the set-up team." She edged closer again. "I've not been with a cupid before. I've heard you are all very ... talented. So ..."

"So ..." He edged back, glanced at Rinna's bedroom door. "Thank you for your help. I'm sure I will be fine."

Dianna gave a little pout, her gaze darting from him to the bedroom door and back. Then she smiled slowly. "Lucky girl. But if you change your mind ..."

"I'll be sure to ring the bell."

Her lips twitched as she placed the bell on the table by the door, bowed and left.

He should get some rest as well. Then go into his mind vault to find the spell. Actually, he'd do that first then rest.

He was just settling on the plush green rug in front of the fire when a sound from the bedroom caught his attention. He rose and rushed to the bedroom door, pressing his ear against it. Korinna was making little noises of distress.

He opened the door to peek in.

The room was stark with barely any furnishings aside from the huge canopied bed she lay in. His gaze arrowed in on her, noting how she twitched, her lips pulled back in a grimace. Sweat glistened on her furrowed brow, her curly hair a spill of black on the white pillow.

A nightmare. Should he wake her? He flicked on the bedside lamp, hoping the light might wake her. It didn't. It just seemed to distress her further. "Wake up, Rinna. You're having a nightmare." He shook her shoulder gingerly.

She grasped his hand – fire shot through him at the point of contact, but he shoved the sensation aside. "Rinna. It's okay. It's only a nightmare. Wake up."

Her eyes fluttered open, gaze sliding around until it

landed on him. "Tam. My Tam. Where did you go? Where did you go?"

"I'm sorry, Rinna. I didn't want to go. But I'm here now. I'm right here."

She tossed her head, her gaze roving around, unseeing. Was she still asleep? "I'm so sorry. I didn't mean to do it. But you weren't here. You weren't here and I hurt so much I missed the signs ... I shouldn't have done it. I shouldn't have done it." She was sobbing now, her body jerking harder with her distress.

He sat on the edge of the bed, pulled her into his arms, stroked her hair. She gripped him hard, burying her head in his chest, sobs racking her body. "Shh, shh. Rinna. It's okay. It's not your fault. I know it's not your fault. Everything's going to be okay. I'm here. I'm here."

"You're here," she said, her sobs abating a little.

"I'm here. I'm always here."

"But you weren't. And now I can never be forgiven." She looked up at him, her eyes a vibrant glowing gold in the semi-dark room – the gold that only showed when she was using her power. But as far as he could tell, she wasn't using it at all. In fact, her power felt ... like there was something horribly wrong with it.

What the Hells was going on here?

He didn't have the chance to ask as she buried her head in his chest, mumbling, "Don't leave me. Please don't leave me."

"I won't," he said, his voice a harsh blade in his throat. "I promise I will never leave you if you need me."

She rubbed her head against him, gripping him more tightly. His arms firmed around her as he shifted his legs onto the bed and laid them both back against the pillows.

As soon as he did, she went completely lax, losing

herself to sleep once more – if she'd ever truly woken from it in the first place. He doubted she had.

Hells.

It seemed she did truly blame herself. But still, the depth of her grief, of her guilt, didn't make sense. Not after all this time. Not when she must know – and Persephone and others must have tried to make her see – that a disaster like Pompeii was something nobody could have prevented, no matter how talented or strong.

Fuck. What exactly had happened to make her punish herself like this?

One thing was certain though: he wasn't going to go anywhere tonight. He'd have to get into his mind vault in the morning after she woke and he could think clearly again. With her in his arms like this, he could think of nothing but her.

Damn, he'd hoped when he couldn't find her that she was happy, safe and fulfilled – even in the depths of his heartbreak, when he'd thought she had dismissed their friendship and forgotten him, he'd wished that. To find out her life was so far from that …

Residing in the Underworld, a permanent treasured guest of Hades and Persephone, didn't even come close to meeting his idea of the life she deserved. He would fulfil his vow to get his mother's powers back and somehow, some way, while he did, he would find a way to make his Rinna happy.

A rumble of thunder followed by a loud knock in the distance told him he'd tied himself to another vow.

He didn't care. He would fulfil them both or die trying. It was the least he owed to the people he loved most in all the Realms.

CHAPTER
FIVE

Korinna woke the next morning warmth blazing along her back, a heavy arm over her waist, the forearm and hand of which she clutched against her breasts. Had she taken someone to bed? She couldn't remember doing so. Hadn't felt any kind of inclination for a sexual partner for a very long time. Perhaps she dreamed. She pinched herself.

"Ow."

The man behind her moved, muttering a little, something hard and jagged poking into her back. But not his cock – although that had firmed a little against her bottom when she moved – but something that lay between her shoulder blades.

It was uncomfortable. She shifted around to see what it was, not caring too much if she woke her bed companion.

"Morning," said a deep, sleep-roughened voice. A voice she knew too well.

"Tam! What are you doing in my bed?" She sat bolt upright, completely dislodging his hold on her, memories of yesterday flooding her mind.

Ah Hells! She'd yelled at him, hit him, argued with him then struck a bargain to help him so she could get the Eleusinian Mysteries Grimoire and a closer look at the HeartsBlood Gem – which still hung around his neck. *It* had been the hard thing poking her in the middle of the back.

She wanted to see the gem, to feel its weight and warmth in her hand, to poke at the magic that lay at its core with the help of Dianna, to uncover its secrets, but right now, her mind kept spiralling to the fact he sat on her bed. And the fact she'd woken up, clutching his arm, spooned against him.

How in everything holy had that happened? What the Hells had happened?

She glanced down, almost sighing in relief when she saw she had her Yummy Sushi pyjamas on – a present from Persephone and Hades on her last birthday in a nod to her Buffy obsession – the TV show the only thing for centuries that Persephone had got her to engage with from the Earthly Realm.

If she was wearing her pyjamas, it meant nothing had happened between them. And he still had his suit on – she couldn't believe Tam wore suits! – although the jacket was missing and the white shirt, looking a little less crisp than it had yesterday, was rolled up at the sleeves to his elbows, showing off the tattoo of an owl on his right forearm.

He still had that? After all this time, it should have worn off, but it looked as fresh as the day she'd put it on him. She touched the matching one hidden under her sleeve, her gaze darting up to his, questioning.

His lips curled in *that* smile again as he gestured at her. "Nice jim-jams."

She pulled the sheet up in front of her. It seemed to

amuse him more, his lips twitching as he edged up onto his elbows.

"They look better on you than they did on Buffy."

"You watch Buffy?"

"Of course." He cocked his brow. "I'm a little surprised you do."

"Why? Why wouldn't I like a show where the kick-arse heroine fights evil and wins the day?"

"Well, when you put it like that ..." He smiled at her, the curve of his lips having a similar effect on her as a caress.

She clutched the sheet tighter. "Why are you in my bed?"

He rubbed one hand over his dark auburn hair, the movement giving her a glimpse of his tanned chest – he'd undone the top buttons on his shirt – and the chain that held the HeartsBlood Gem. Her mouth dried. He looked deliciously dishevelled sitting on her bed, his hair spiked up now in a sexy just-awake kind of way, his jaw covered with a red-tinted five o'clock shadow – a far cry from the suave, suited stranger she'd been so angry with yesterday. She tried to ignore the way his dishevelment made him even more handsome and raised her brows – a look he used to call 'haughty Rinna'. "Well? Why are you here?"

"You asked me to stay. You were having a nightmare."

Oh crap. She hoped she hadn't talked in her sleep. She looked more closely at him. He didn't look like he was appalled, or pitied her. He looked his usual self. Well, not quite his usual self. He'd been a young cupid of fifty when they first met – the human equivalent of about fifteen or sixteen – and had left her just as he'd entered his demi-God manhood at one-hundred years old.

His face was even handsomer now than it had been back then, his unruly auburn hair cut short at the back and sides with just enough at the top to sit up without the help of product – not flop all over his forehead like it once had. His indigo eyes were even more vivid than she remembered – probably something to do with the increase in power emanating from his every pore. And he'd filled out. Her fingers tingled as she remembered the sensation of the wiry muscles of the forearm she'd clutched in sleep, the taut strength of the chest and stomach muscles she'd nestled against last night. She had a vague memory of doing that, of holding him tight and not letting go.

How embarrassing! What must he think of her? She swung away from him, intending to get off the bed, make an excuse about needing to get dressed. She needed to find her anger again: it was her only armour against him.

But he touched her arm before she could get off the bed and she froze as a tsunami of sensation flooded through her – ye Gods! How could he still make her feel like this?

"Rinna. Are you okay?"

She glanced back over her shoulder. He blinked, his gaze roving over her in a way that made her tingle low in her belly, a sensation that heralded an earthquake of trembling deep in her core.

She leaped to her feet. "Fine. I'm fine. Very rested. Thanks for helping with the ..." She waved at the bed. "Nightmares."

"My pleasure." He smiled, that slow curl of lips on one side that made a dimple pop out.

The tremors went up a notch on the Richter scale. How could this be happening? She was angry with him. Wasn't she?

"Are you sure you're okay?"

"Fine." Had she just squeaked? She cleared her throat, spoke deeply. "Fine."

His lips twitched. "Good. I'm glad." He swung his legs around and over the side of the bed. As he moved, a darkly red shadow under the crumpled white of his shirt caught her attention. The HeartsBlood Gem. How could she have forgotten about it?

She wanted to see it again.

Her fingers brushed against the hot skin at his collar as she reached for the chain.

He stilled. She stilled.

Slowly, their gazes met.

He swallowed hard. "Rinna."

"Yes," she breathed. She stood in between his legs, the warmth of him wrapping around her. Ye Gods. The trembling tightened, tightened: an eight on the Richter scale; a nine ...

He leaned up. She leaned down.

The door opened with a loud squeak.

Korinna jumped away from Tam as Dianna walked in, a tray in her hands. "Breakfast is prepared at Lady Persephone's request ... Oh, sorry, did I interrupt something?"

"No." She couldn't even look at him. "Tam was just showing me his gem."

Dianna's lips twitched as she walked closer, her gaze roving over him salaciously. "I bet he was."

"Not like that!" Korinna blustered, her face hotter than Satan's fires. "The HeartsBlood Gem. Show her, Tam."

He grinned as he pulled it out slowly from beneath his shirt, playing up to Dianna, who had put the tray down to say, "Oh my," while she fanned her face, her gaze not on the gem, but lower. Embarrassment gave way to a spark of anger, which quickly devolved into self-pity. Dianna made flirting look so easy. As a Soteira should. As she'd somehow never been able to do.

Not that she wanted to know how to flirt with Tam. That would be completely inappropriate. Particularly as she hated him. Was mad at him. Furious really. No amount of Richter-scale trembling could make her forget that. So no need to want to flirt or anything like it. And definitely no need to keep thinking about the way his gaze had dipped to her lips as he'd leaned towards her before Dianna had barged in. Or the way she'd woken. Warm and ruffled from sleeping. In his arms. All night.

Or how she'd almost orgasmed standing between his legs as they'd looked at each other.

Oh Hells. She wanted to fan herself, but then, that would give away too much. Wouldn't it?

Yes, yes, it would. Not to mention, she wouldn't look sexy like Dianna did – eyes sparking flirtatiously, her entire body screaming she'd be up for sex if it was on offer.

Was it?

Her gaze darted to Tam.

He no longer looked at Dianna as he held the Hearts-Blood Gem out of his shirt. His gaze was fixed firmly on her.

Her face flamed to volcanic levels in less than a second. Why now? Why Tam?

She reached for the glass on her bedside stand, desperate to have an excuse to look away and hide herself for a moment – suddenly horribly aware of the fact she was in pyjamas, her dark hair a wild mess of curls falling every-where. Dianna, with her sweep of long, glossy blonde hair and slinky black party dress and heals, looked far sexier without trying than Korinna had ever managed.

She gulped down the cooling water. It helped, but not as much as if she could tip it over her head, or bury her face in it.

Satan and all his devils be damned. This morning was

not going like she meant it to. Not that it was entirely her fault. *I mean, I didn't ask Tam to come to my bed. Well, I did. But not like that. And I certainly never intended to sleep with him.*

An image of rolling around naked in the bed with him imprinted itself in her mind. A little gasp escaped her mouth.

"Rinna – are you okay?"

He was there in front of her again suddenly, the gem she should be concentrating on glittering as it swung against his chest. But she couldn't seem to focus on it. Only on his brilliant indigo eyes and their framing of long dark lashes. Those eyes glowed as he touched her, as he looked down at her. His voice buzzed in her ear. She looked at his lips as they moved over words of concern. All she wanted to do was put her thumb in the divot right in the middle of his bottom lip. Then she'd like to follow up with her tongue.

"Ye Gods!" she muttered. This was insane. Why was this happening to her? It never had before. Maybe it had something to do with the gem. Yes. That must be it. It was said to be a piece of the Goddess Vesta's heart – she was the Goddess of Hearth and Home but also fecundity. Maybe there was a little something sexy, a little something naughty, locked inside the depths of the gem that spoke to her; made her feel like this. Maybe it had unlocked the sensuality that was supposed to be part of her Soteira nature.

It made more sense than the alternative. That she wasn't furious at Tam. That she …

She groaned again, not wanting to put words to the feelings inside her. It would make them too real – whether they were influenced by the gem or not.

His hands tightened on her shoulders at her groan. She wished he'd let go.

"You don't feel dizzy again, do you? Perhaps you should rest some more? Or eat? Dianna – bring that tray over here."

"No, no, I'm fine. It's not that," she managed to say, her voice so dry, as if she'd swallowed salt and sand rather than water only moments ago. "I'm rested enough." Her entire body sang with energy in a way it never had before. Ye Gods. Was this desire? It felt nothing like what she'd felt the times she'd taken a bed mate – primarily to get Persephone and Hades off her back about not living a full life. And also, because the scholar side of her wanted to see what she'd been missing. All the other Soteira made such a fuss over how great sex was. But after trying a dozen bed mates over a few centuries – she'd needed a reasonable selection to gather the relevant data – she'd come to the conclusion that, despite having been brought up as one of them, she wasn't a true Soteira. Not surprising given she'd been taken in by Demeter as a kindness when her mother had died, her mother having been friends with the Goddess. Nobody knew who her father was – her mother took that secret to the grave. I was partly why she'd been quite content to believe she just wasn't that into sex ... until now. So why had she made such a massive mistake?

Maybe the problem was her sample group hadn't been big enough. Or maybe they just hadn't been good enough. They certainly had never made her feel like this just by gripping her shoulders and staring solemnly down at her. And none of them had ever smelled like Tam; like lemons and sandalwood and the wildness of the sea – how that could be a scent, she wasn't sure, but it was the perfect description for the elusive aroma that teased her and made her ache.

He was staring at her. He'd asked her a question. What was it? Ah yes ... was she rested. "Plenty rested," she choked out.

"But you're trembling."

"Ah ... hungry. Need food."

"Yes. Of course. Dianna?" He helped her sit on the bed as Dianna went to place the tray next to her.

Korinna popped up before the tray hit the mattress. "Ah, not here." She couldn't sit in bed and eat with Tam watching her. Remembering all over again how she'd woken. "I don't like eating in bed."

"It's hardly in bed ..." Tam began, but she was already out the door, heading towards the table – where she could sit at one end and he could sit way down the other end as far from her as possible.

CHAPTER
SIX

Korinna fell into her seat and gestured to the one at the other end of the table for Tam. He glanced at it, brow cocked, but then headed towards it.

"Don't sit down there." Dianna – the traitor! – put the tray down in front of Korinna and pulled the chair out catty-corner to her. "It's much easier for everyone – namely me," she said, pursing her lips and touching her hair, "if you sit down here. Then I won't have to wear out my pretties traipsing between you both." She waved at her hot pink strappy stilettos.

Korinna eyed her friend's outfit. "I thought you were supposed to go in a costume to the party."

"I am in costume. I'm Samantha from Sex in the City." She rolled her eyes at Korinna when she just stared. "You know – sex on legs, wears LBDs and stilettos." She cocked her brow at Tam. "I was hoping I could sell it."

"You certainly do that," Tam said as he took his seat.

"LBD?" Korinna asked, jaw tight.

"Little Black Dress," Tam answered, reaching for the coffee pot.

Of course he would know that. She glanced down at her friend's feet again. "They look like little torture machines. Why would you wear them at all?"

"I love my Louboutins – they're so pretty. And they do such great things for my calf muscles." She did a little turn to show off her legs.

Korinna shook her head and chuckled. "Maybe you should give them over to Hades to use on his worst offenders. A couple of centuries wearing them would be the best punishment ever."

Dianna took a step back, hand to her chest. "Sacrilege! You will not even suggest such a thing to our lord. He might just do it and then I'd be without my pretties."

"You are ridiculous, you know," Korinna said to her friend.

"At least I'm ridiculous with pretty shoes. Right, Tamuel? I see from your suit you're a man who enjoys fashion."

He nodded. "I am. And your shoes are lovely. And certainly shouldn't be wasted serving us. You should go to the party now."

Her pale blue eyes glowed. "Really? If you're sure? I could always stay a little longer to see to your every need." She winked as she stepped back from the table.

He didn't respond. In fact, his gaze was on Korinna, not Dianna. Strange. Not only would most men be begging at Dianna's feet about now, he was a cupid. Playful flirting was his thing. Pity she'd realised that too late when they were younger. Frowning, she said, "We'll call if we need anything." She didn't need Dianna to help her investigate the gem's magic. At least, not while Tam was here. "Have fun at the party."

"Thank you. You're the best, Kor." Dianna kissed her on

the cheek before turning to Tam. "Ring if you need anything." She draped her hand on his shoulder. "Anything at all." Then she spun in a circle and disappeared in a cloud of pink and lavender.

He waved his hand, coughing a little. "Someone should tell your friend she needs to work on her exit magic."

Korinna snorted. "Oh, I think it worked exactly as she wanted it to." There were now pink and lavender sparkles shining in Tam's auburn hair. Korinna's fingers tingled with the need to brush them off. Her friend couldn't lay claim to him! He was hers first.

She blinked, pulling her hand back into her lap, fingers curling in so hard, her fingernails bit into her palm.

Tam wasn't hers. He'd never been hers. It was best she remember that.

She glared at him as he brushed the sparkles off his shirt. He glanced up, a rueful smile on his face. She quickly looked at the tray, grabbing the first thing that came to hand.

"Umm, since when do you like bacon?" Tam asked.

"Since forever." Instead of putting it on her plate, she bit into it and chewed, swallowed.

"Do you want some more?" he asked, lips twitching as he watched her.

She forced herself to swallow the last bit, managing not to dry retch at the salty-fatty taste left in her mouth. She couldn't let him know she'd been so distracted as to pick it up in the first place. He'd want to know why and that was a question she did not want to answer. No way, no how. She smiled brightly at him and waved away the plate. "No, it's fine. You take the rest. I know how much you love it."

"Who doesn't love bacon, right?"

"Absolutely." Her smile slipped as he tucked in. She

grabbed the cranberry juice, pouring herself a large glass and swallowed it down in one go. The tartness helped rid her of the taste of bacon. Blech. Horrid stuff.

Tam had always teased her about her hatred of bacon – he'd said it was unnatural. Perhaps it was. But then, many things about her had never been quite right, had they? This was just one more thing.

She turned her attention to the rest of the tray. Eggs, scrambled as she liked them; sourdough toast, lightly golden; a bowl of fresh berries – strawberries, blackberries and blueberries, her favourites; and a couple of croissants and jam. She frowned a little as she spooned some eggs onto toast. There was way too much food here for one person.

Oh! Dianna's surprise when she'd caught Tam in Korinna's room this morning had been fake. But how had she known he was there?

That was when she spied the door, slightly ajar, on the opposite side of her room. Where had that come from? Her suite comprised of this living and study area, her bedroom and an ensuite. There wasn't another room off it. Why would Hades have added a room—

Persephone! She'd obviously asked Hades to create a room for Tam to stay in as part of her suite. Why on earth would they do that? They had never situated any other interview subjects near her suite, let alone created another room that led right off her living area.

What in all the Hells was Seph up to? And was Tam in on it?

She gave him the side-eye. He didn't notice, too taken with his breakfast to do more than stop to breathe. A smile flickered, unbidden, on her lips. He had always loved breakfast the most of any meal, even when the fare had been minimal through various parts of their training. Perhaps he'd been hungriest then. She'd never asked. But it had always been enjoyable watching how he tucked into the food they were given to break their fast. He always ate like there was no tomorrow. But then again, he'd kind of lived like that too. At least, he had when she'd known him. A cupid version of a mid-teen terror when he'd first moved to the mountain camp, he'd been turning into the grown-up version before he'd disappeared.

Her smile faded.

Anger returned. And a terrible sadness along with it.

She pushed at the sadness, grabbing at the anger, wanting it to fill her. But the sadness remained. She had to get over it though. She needed to go with him to visit Clodia, especially given they had the gem. The ancient witch was rumoured to know things about the ancient Gods and even more ancient magics that lay at the heart of the very spell she wanted to use from the Eleusinian Mysteries Grimoire. Talking to the Vestal High Priestess would bring her one step closer to completing her vow. Which meant, she would have to spend up to a week with him. She could rope in these wayward emotions and desires to get what she wanted. She *would* rope them in. It wasn't like he could return her feelings after all; he was a cupid and she was ... well, her – a useless, damaged witch of unspecified heritage who didn't deserve love after what she'd done.

He glanced up at her, smiled. "I missed this."

His words, that look, made her want to cry, but instead, she nodded and gave her attention to her breakfast.

"I'm surprised you haven't jumped me yet."

"What?" Rinna's head snapped up. The spoonful of eggs on the way to her mouth dropped, landing with a splat on the edge of her plate, spraying across the table and spattering her Yummy Sushi pyjamas. She didn't seem to notice as she stared at him, her big topaz eyes widening, a stain of red painting her cheeks. "I wouldn't ... I didn't ..."

For a moment, Tamuel wanted to tease her for misunderstanding his words, but the need died as fast as it came. He had never been able to stand to see her pained in any way. So, rather than teasing, he gestured to the gem hanging against his chest. "For this. I thought you'd be more interested in looking at it than eating breakfast."

"Oh, I ... um ... Yes. Of course. I am. Very interested." She picked up her spoon, staring at the mess she'd made on the table and her pyjamas. "Oh, I'm sorry. Did any get on you?"

"None. But it did get on you." He waved a hand. Magic prickled in the air and the mess disappeared.

She swallowed hard. "Impressive."

"Hardly." It was the kind of simple spell she'd mastered long before they'd begun their training – where he'd struggled for a long time, his cupid and warlock powers not seeming to play well with one another. Until she'd befriended him and begun to help and they'd discovered their powers had a certain symbiosis together, hers helping to rope in his and allow him to get a handle on them; his feeding into hers, allowing her to do more complicated spells than she should have been able to at such a young age – an indication of the promise of the powerful magical practitioner she was bound to become. And it had grown. He sensed it before he even entered her room yesterday. Her power was a tang on the air, a constant vibration emanating from her skin, glowing in her eyes. But there was a strange wrongness about it. Was the wrongness why she hadn't used it to clean up such a simple mess?

And come to think of it, why had Dianna been so

concerned with making certain Rinna had everything she needed? Surely someone with as much power as Rinna had in her little finger could summon anything she wanted? He half-expected her to click her fingers and call the Hearts-Blood Gem to her. And yet, hands clenched in her lap, she asked, "Can you tell me how you came to get it? All the rumours I tracked down said it was used by the Vestal High Priestess Clodia and then lost with her when she disappeared."

He focused on her question – his could wait until she was more comfortable with him again. "It didn't disappear. It was tied into the garden of the Vestal Temple in Roma where Clodia laid her curse to take my mother's Goddess-given power for her own. She used it to amplify her magics to place the curse and channel the power into herself from my mother."

"What a misuse of its power."

He nodded. "Yes. We think that misuse was why her spell backfired. Rather than transferring the powers to Clodia, it transmuted them, pushing them down deep inside my mother, attached to her eternal soul. Her powers travelled with her through her incarnations but she wasn't able to use them because the transmutation had the unfortunate side-effect of energising Clodia's curse, like a battery."

"Why would it do that?"

"Protective magic gone haywire? Clodia couldn't take my mother's powers as long as they were hidden inside her and the HeartsBlood Gem hid itself where it was last used until I found it. We planned to use it to reverse the curse, but Clodia had also been tied to the area." He told her of what had happened, of how they had almost lost everything until her mother sacrificed the power that should have been hers to open the rift into the Void and pushed Clodia there. The powers had disappeared into the Void with the evil priestess-witch.

"I vowed that night to do everything I could to get my mother's powers back. I've been following every lead for the last eight months. I managed to find out Hades and Zeus took Clodia from the Void and put her in Tartarus as punishment, but the power wasn't with her. I tried everything I knew to open the Void to search for it, but nothing worked. Only the most extreme burst of power will tear it open. And I don't have access to that kind of power."

"Why didn't you ask a God or Goddess to open it for you?"

"You know their feelings on entering the Void. Hades and Zeus only did it because they were furious with Clodia and wanted to personally punish her. There was no way they would open it for me. Besides which, I realised, even if I got in, I wouldn't have a clue how to go about finding where the powers are. The Void is, for all intents and purposes, endless after all. So, my only chance is to speak with Clodia. She's opened the Void before, so must know how to gain the power to do so. I also need her to tell me how not to get lost in there, how to find the powers and then get out again with them intact."

"And you need the gem to speak to Clodia?"

His fingers closed around the blood-red stone. "She is tied to it in the same way my mother is. I think I can use it to get the answers I need, but also, to transfer the power from wherever it is back into my mother when I find it. But while there was a lot of research – primarily yours – that stated it could be used in this way, there was nothing to tell me exactly how. Nothing I've done has made it react in any way since Jules gave it to me."

"Of course it didn't. The gem, whether it is truly a piece of a Goddess' heart or not, was created by a Goddess aligned with mother nature. Its spells and power can only be untapped by a female with a like power."

"That makes sense. Although, if that's the case, then how am I to use it?"

"You'd need a female to help you use it. Although, given you inherited some of your powers from your mother, you most likely will only need the witch to act as a channel and not use her actual powers. It probably would have worked for you if your mother had just held it with you." She frowned. "But she should have known that if she'd held the gem even after she lost her powers – the gem would be happy to whisper its secrets to her. Why isn't she here with you?"

"Because I didn't tell her what I was doing when I asked for the gem."

"What?"

"She would never have agreed with my plan and would have tried to make me take back my vow. She says she's perfectly happy with her lot." He shook his head. "But I know she can't be. Not when it means she won't get to live forever with her soulmate, my father. Not when her human death will lead to his. I see the sadness in her, feel the pain of the loss that is to come in knowing her death will snuff both their lights from this world. And I can't ... I have to ..."

She placed her hand over his as he shook his head, words failing him. Her lips trembled a little, eyes full of an empathy he'd not felt from anyone but her in all his long years.

For a long, timeless moment, they stared at each other, hands gripping, her beautiful eyes on his, knowing, understanding; just as she'd done so many times when they'd been friends. It comforted him, wrapping him in warmth. He eased forward, his hand coming up to cup her face. "Rinna."

She turned her head, lips finding his palm; warm, her breath slightly damp as she pressed a kiss into his skin. Her eyes closed, long lashes a sweep of darkness against too-pale cheeks.

He held his breath, wanting her to stay where she was and yet move closer.

Her eyes opened, she looked up at him.

A punch in the heart, the stark want there. "Rinna," he whispered again.

An alarm peeled through the silence – the chronometer.

The sound broke the spell – of him, of her, of them. She jerked away, her chair skidding back, the nasty squawk vying with the alarm.

He blinked. Looked up at her. She seemed to be as shocked by what had almost happened as him. "Rinna ..." he began.

The chronometer beeped, a voice replacing the shrill alarm: *"The veil is thinning. Alignment adjusting ... adjusting ... The Underworld's position has changed. Time has shifted. One week in the Underworld is now equal to two hours in the Earthly Realm. The clocks will strike twelve on All Hallows' Eve in one and a half weeks Tartarus time. Allotted time lost: two and a half weeks. Alignment still changing. Further alarms will be forthcoming."*

He stared at the chronometer to verify the words he still couldn't believe. "Shit."

"You used my voice? How? Why?"

He looked up, met her confused gaze. "I pulled it out of my memory vault – I missed you. Besides, something about the specs reminded me of you. I should have known you designed it."

They stared at each other for a long moment until she blinked, took a step back. Cleared her throat. "Umm, well, we should get going before you run out of more time."

"You want to come?"

Her lips quirked. "You don't think I'm going to let you go wandering through the Underworld and into Tartarus alone, do you? You don't know anything about all the nasties down there that could stop you from getting to Clodia's cell."

"Isn't the Hells-Key supposed to help with that?"

She picked at her cuticles as she stared him down. "It doesn't shield from everything. And the Underworld will fight you all the way, especially if you don't know what you're doing."

"And you do? I got the impression you never leave these suites."

Another shrug. "I've been out. When I need to talk to an interview subject. You need me to go with you. Not to mention, you need my help to work the gem."

"You could tell me what I need to know now. And I could ask Dianna or one of the other Soteira to come with me. You don't have to come if you don't want to." What was he doing, giving her an out? He wanted her to come.

"Don't you want me to come with you?"

"I do ... I just ... I thought, after you believed I left and didn't write, that you wouldn't want to spend more time with me than absolutely necessary."

Her mouth worked for a moment and she looked down at her lap. "About that ... I ... I ... Maybe there is something to what you say about someone inter- cepting our letters." She cleared her throat, glanced up at him again. "Besides, I want to speak with Clodia myself."

He stared at her, expecting her to look away, but she didn't. Despite all the changes, the spark of the girl he'd once known was still within her. "Okay."

"Okay?"

He shrugged. "It makes more sense. We can save time by discussing the gem and the spells we might need to use as we travel. Now that I've lost a few weeks, it seems like the best option."

"Oh. Of course."

Was that a flash of hurt in her eyes? Damn, he didn't mean to make her feel rejected – he just didn't want his eagerness to show too much. He leaned forward, stilled her fingers as they clenched in her lap. Her gaze met his, boring into him as she frowned a little. He wanted to kiss that frown away. He swallowed hard. "And it will give us time to discuss what happened after Eros took me. And maybe, we can make plans to find out why someone meddled after ..."

"After?"

"After we've finished here."

She looked down, the dark sweep of her lashes against the shadows under her eyes doing all sorts of things inside him – things he gathered close, not wanting her to see. No point in spooking her by the violence of his feelings. She could never love him back in the same way.

"Okay."

"So, you want to find out who kept those letters from us after we finish this?"

Her smile faded, replaced by shadows in her eyes. "One thing at a time," she whispered.

He nodded quickly. "One thing at a time."

She stood. "So ..." She cleared her throat. "I should go

get changed and attach the Hells-Key. You need to do the same – that suit will get wrecked down in the tunnels."

"Dianna said there's clothes for me in the room."

"Good. Umm ... see you back here in a few hours."

"It will take you that long to get changed?"

She smirked, eyes glinting. "I see you are as yet to read the instructions for the Hells-Key. You'll need some recovery time."

He grimaced. "Does it hurt?"

Her lips curled into a small smile. "Not as much as you think it would given you have to attach it to your chest. But it does take something out of you." She backed up a few more steps. "I'll see you when you're ready."

"Okay. I'll ..." She'd already disappeared into her room, the heavy carved black doors slamming shut behind her. He let out a sigh. "Well, that went better than expected." She'd forgiven him – maybe – and she was helping him, so he would have more time to make certain that forgiveness stuck and maybe they could start up their friendship again. Life would be much more tolerable with Rinna in it.

He only hoped the Hells-Key spell wasn't as painful as she'd made it sound – although, considering Hades created them, it was probably going to be worse.

CHAPTER
SEVEN

Tamuel glanced at Korinna as she marched stoically by his side. She seemed nervous – shoulders held tightly, eyes darting around. Not that he blamed her. The journey was proving to be difficult. More difficult than he'd thought it would be with Hades' Hells-Key melted into his chest.

He touched the still-throbbing place where the Hells-Key had magically become a part of him half a day ago. By all the Realms, it had hurt.

He glanced at Rinna again, spying the red skin showing above the V of her dark grey, long-sleeved Soteira tunic. She seemed unphased by it. Yet his powers were still sparking and fighting it every step, not wanting to accept what was basically death magic anywhere near it. Rinna had been right – it had knocked him for six and he'd lost consciousness for over an hour. Then it had taken him another hour to stop his limbs from shaking so badly he couldn't even stand, let alone get changed. The upshot of which was he still hadn't gone into his mind vault to retrieve the memory of the sigil. A problem for when they returned.

He frowned down at the witch at his side. "Do you wear the Hells-Key a lot?" That would explain why she wasn't affected by the magic of attaching it.

"No. I don't need it most of the time – only when I want to interview a soul who's down here that Hades can't bring to his palace for reasons of security. Why?" She glanced up at him, grimaced. "Still feeling it, aren't you? We could have waited a little longer – the chronometer hasn't gone off again and according to the map, the path to the Gates of Tartarus will only take us a few days at the moment."

"How long after that to Clodia's cell?"

She shrugged. "The map won't show us until we step into Tartarus. The Underworld and Hell Realms are too large to put on a hundred-thousand maps let alone one." She showed him the map. "This has been spelled to show the most direct route."

"Kind of like Google Maps."

"Google Maps?"

He shook his head. "Never mind. So it tells you how long the journey will be?"

"There is an indicator here." She pointed at an hour-glass image where the sand shifted from the top bowl to the bottom. "However, because things constantly shift and change down here, it's never certain how long a journey will take." She glanced up at him again. "I wish we could stop so you could rest but now we're in the tunnels ..." She looked around them. "It's best not to stop."

"I don't need to rest." He waved his hand, not wanting to show weakness in front of her – he'd just got her trusting him again, after all. "I was wondering how come the Hells-Key didn't affect you like it did me?"

"Oh. Probably because it's not fighting against my magic."

"Why not?" It should have, given her magic was one of life and healing.

"I ... don't use my magic."

"What? Why?"

She shrugged nonchalantly, but something about the way she held her shoulders told him she was the opposite. "I just prefer to do things without it. I've not used it for a long time."

"But I can feel it."

Her gaze darted up to him. "That's not possible. I keep it locked down."

He waved his hand at her. "Well, you're not doing a very good job because it's all over you. You're glowing with it."

Fear sharpened her features as she looked down at herself. "I'm not."

"You are."

She looked up at him, eyes pained, pleading. "You're lying."

He couldn't stand that look in her eyes, so he smiled. "You're not glowing," he lied. She wasn't lighting up the tunnel, but her skin shone like it was moon-struck. Maybe he could see it because of the way their powers had always worked together. A thought to delve into another time.

"Then why did you say you could?"

"What I meant was that I can feel it in you, like a vibration deep down."

She took in a shuddering breath. "I'll have to tighten my shielding. Sorry if it's worrying you."

"I'm not worried. I always liked your magic. It's soothing."

She frowned up at him. "It's hardly that."

He wanted to press her but she flicked the map and stared down at it. "We need to take the next left."

He glanced at the map she insisted she be in charge of. He'd wanted to tease her about being a bossy-boots but the words caught in his mouth as she'd raked her glossy curls into a knot on the top of her head, told him to grab his backpack – she'd packed it for him while he was out of commission – and walked out the door.

"Wouldn't that right path get us there faster?"

"It would, except ..." She tapped the tunnel that led off from it. "We'd have to go through the Banshee Hall – and trust me, you don't want to go there. Those girls can talk your head off."

She shook her head, a lock of hair falling down to kiss the skin of her neck. He wanted to brush it aside. Place his lips there instead.

His mouth dried. He coughed.

"Here." She folded the map up under her arm, then pulled a metal bottle out of the backpack he wore and handed it to him. "I packed a few bottles of water for each of us and some food – I didn't know how long we'd be gone and it isn't wise to eat anything you might be offered in the halls or tunnels of the Underworld or Tartarus."

"So I've heard," he rasped, his mouth as dry and hot as ... Well, Hell. He chuckled to himself then took a quick chug of the water. It went down too fast, making him cough and splutter.

She slapped his back. "Easy. We could be down here for days and you don't want to use up all your water before we're done."

"I am a cupid. I can do without food or water for some time."

"You've never tried to do so in the Underworld though, have you? Time isn't the only thing that's different down here. Speaking of which, what does your chronometer say?"

He glanced down at it. "The alignment hasn't changed."

"You have to take your time from Australian Eastern Standard time?"

He nodded. "I cast the spell that allowed me to come down here in corporeal form in the Coven library under my parent's Melbourne mansion."

"Weren't you worried they'd feel what you were doing and try to stop you?"

"Of course." His parents would never have let him take this risk. "I made certain they'd left for the Coven's Halloween party before I opened the portal from the library – nobody but my mum would come down there after hours, so among other considerations, it was the safest place to punch a hole through the weakening veil."

"I still don't understand how you managed to make the portal open. The spell from the Mysteries Grimoire must have taken huge amounts of magical energies to keep you corporeal and let you open the portal that brought you to Hades' Palace. How did it not burn you up?"

He cocked his brow. "That was the easy part. I used other magic to help power the spell."

Her brow furrowed more deeply, the look of consternation on her face bringing back memories of how she always looked when she was stumped. He wanted to run his finger down that groove and smooth it away, but put aside the urge as she asked, "How? That kind of magic doesn't just lie around waiting to be used. You were alone, so you couldn't syphon off power from anyone else, even if you had a want to do such a thing."

"I never said I was alone. I just said my parents weren't there."

"But even if you syphoned someone's power with permission, it wouldn't be enough. Not for you."

"Why'd you say that?"

"Well, that's not exactly how your powers work – you were always more of a giver than a taker. With me at least." She blushed, frown deepening.

"You're right, I didn't do that."

She nodded briskly. "As I said. And I know you didn't use the HeartsBlood Gem given you've been unable to use it. So, how did you do it?"

He blinked, lost in her eyes again as she stared up at him. "What?"

"Get here? Without the help of the HeartsBlood Gem. How did you get enough power to make the spell work?"

"Umm ..." He shot her a quick smile to cover his lapse in concentration. "Well, my mother's Coven have managed to build up quite a collection of grimoires and books on magic – both light and dark. Over the years, as Coven members have died, many of their spirits have stayed around to help guard and look over the connection. An underground chamber, the size of many football fields, was built on top of a couple of main lay-lines, with Stevens House constructed on top to conceal the entrance from unwanted eyes. It houses the Melbourne Coven's library as well as the Stevens' private collection. My mother, Jules, and my great-grandmama, Violetta, are the archivist and librarian and they continue to build and add to it."

"Making it the perfect place for your spell. I get it. But that still doesn't explain where you got the excess power to drive the spell. The power reserves for a spell like this to not only break through the veil, but allow you entry into the Death Realms while alive and corporeal are enormous. I mean, Hades himself had to bring me and the other Soteira down here and used considerable magics to do so – and while you are powerful, you're no son of a Titan."

"Yes. Well, there was also the power the Stevens' spirits gave me."

She frowned. "That might gain you enough, but only if you fully drained them." She gripped his arm, eyes widening, worry flickering there. "You didn't, did you?"

"Of course not. I would never use a spirit that way. Besides, they are too important to my family and I would never do anything to cause Mum and Dad more pain."

"Of course." She let out a shuddering breath, letting go of his arm.

It was his turn to frown – why did the thought of using up spirits like that so affect her? True, it was an evil thing to do – as evil as draining another magic user's powers without permission – but this felt more ... personal than an issue of morals. Did this have something to do with what happened to bring her here? What the fuck had happened at Pompeii? Was it more than the natural disaster they'd all been told it was? He didn't get a chance to ask, because, as her gaze met his once more, the words were lost to him.

"So ..." she said, clearing her throat and looking away. "The magic you've told me about so far would be enough to open the portal but it wouldn't be enough to keep you corporeal so you could bring the HeartsBlood Gem with you and then close the portal behind you cleanly."

Her shoulder brushed against his arm. Sparks shivered through him, making his cock twitch. He really wished she'd stop touching him so casually like that – especially given his cock didn't seem to know the meaning of a simple friendly touch from her. Thankfully, she didn't notice his pause.

She spun to face him on a gasp, continuing to walk backwards. "Don't tell me you left the portal open? Do you know how dangerous that could be? Anyone could stumble on it and fall through – or find their way from here to there."

He smiled down at her, her concern a balm. "I wasn't that stupid. The portal closed behind me."

She pressed her lips together, that little frown of consternation making his lips twitch as she said, "Then how?"

"Well, what I didn't tell you before about my mother is that she was allergic to magic."

"What? How is that possible when she had all that magic repressed inside her?"

"Remember I said how the protective magic went awry?" She nodded. "Well, we think that it, in conjunction with the HeartsBlood Gem, in an effort to keep her safe from further machinations against her, made her hyper-sensitive to magic."

"Another way to stop Clodia – or anyone else – from trying to steal the powers. It was the ultimate shield."

He nodded. "Yes, because the upshot was that her reaction to magic could be explosive to others. Unfortunately, it was also explosive to her."

"Bugger."

"Indeed. However, her work as the Coven's archivist – one of the most talented they've had in centuries – meant they had to do something about that little issue so she could work in a library full of magical books, grimoires and manuscripts."

A light lit her eye. "They created an ark, didn't they?"

He smiled brightly at her. "How did you guess?"

"It's the only option. Where did they put it?"

"Violetta created it and placed it in a secret cavern under the library that only the family spirits know is there."

"That amount of power ... it's incredibly dangerous. Surely she syphoned it off regularly."

He shook his head. "There wasn't anywhere she could syphon it too that wouldn't affect my mum. So she just kept making the ark larger."

Her mouth dropped open. "You tapped into that?"

He nodded, smiling widely. "It was quite a ride." She slapped his arm. "Ow! What was that for?"

"Do you realise how stupidly reckless that was? You could have killed yourself! Or set the entire building down on your head!" Her voice echoed sharply in the dark tunnel. "You could have caused an earthquake. Innocents could have been killed!"

"But I didn't," he said, grabbing her hand before she could hit him again.

She was trembling.

"Hey, hey, it's okay." He grasped her shoulders, stopped walking. "Nothing happened. The spell worked as it should and now I'm here with you, no worse for wear. Well, except for the bruising – you really know how to pack a punch." She didn't smile at his funning as she would have in the past. He brushed a wisp of hair from her cheek with his knuckles, too aware of the lemon and spice scent of her as it rose around him. He let go of her shoulder to cup her face. She still trembled, the shadow of something horrible flickering in her eyes.

He hated seeing it. Wanted to make that terrible look of loss just go away.

He leaned a little closer; her breath brushed against his cheeks. His gaze dipped to her lips. She bit into the lower one. He wanted to put his lips there, stop her from doing that. But first, he needed to find out why she was like this. It couldn't wait until later.

Pulling back a little, he asked, "Rinna, what happened at Pompeii? You know it wasn't your fault, right?"

She stared at him for long, silent seconds. Her mouth opened a little. He thought she was going to tell him.

His chronometer's alarm went off, screeching in the air for a few seconds that made them clap their hands to their ears, both their gazes going to the dial. It spun and shifted, the arms and gears clacking and whirring as the alarm cut off and her voice said, *"The veil is thinning. Alignment adjusting ... computing, computing ... The Underworld's position has changed. Time has shifted. One day in the Underworld is now equal to fifteen minutes in the Earthly Realm. The clocks will strike twelve on All Hallows' Eve in six days Tartarus time. Allotted time lost since last computation: five days. Alignment still changing. Further alarms will be forthcoming."*

"Shit." It was changing faster than he thought it would, even with Persephone's warnings that this All Hallows' Eve would be different.

"Something's not right," Rinna said quietly, her gaze still on the chronometer. "The Underworld should be moving further away from the Earthly Realm this All Hallows' Eve, not closer. It's not due to take that position for another fifty years, Earthly Realm time."

"Ah, I forgot to tell you." He told her about Persephone's warning.

"Why didn't you tell me before now?"

"Would it have made a difference?"

"Yes ... No ... I don't know. But I don't like to be left in the dark."

"That wasn't my intention."

She stared at him for long moments, biting her lip. "It will be okay. We still have time. We just have to hurry."

"And we weren't hurrying already?"

Her mouth quirked. "Not really." She glanced down at the map.

"Rinna?"

She looked up at him. "I just ... now that you're here ... I didn't want it to be over too quickly. I ... I missed you."

"I missed you too." His hands were somehow on her face again, his fingers stroking her cheeks. He wanted to kiss her, but he also still wanted to know what had happened to her. "Rinna ..." The earth rumbled around them, making him stumble a step and let go. "What now?"

She glanced around, worry making her frown deepen. "We shouldn't have stopped." She turned to him, her hand slipping easily into his, tugging him into a walk. "We have to go."

"What are you talking about?"

"I know better than to stop in the tunnels. I shouldn't have indulged my need to ..." The ground rumbled and tipped again, making them stumble back half a dozen steps. He grabbed a hold of her to steady her, but she was rock solid. More so than him. "Don't. We can't stop."

"But we're not finished here yet."

"Yes, we are. We don't have time for this." She jerked out of his hold, grabbed his hand again and pulled him into a brisk walk as earth around them rumbled, showering them in dirt.

He raised a shield bubble over them to protect them, then swung in front of her, making her stop, look up at him. He cupped her face again. "I always have time for you, Rinna. Always. And I want to know what happened to you. I want to know how I can help."

"Why?"

"I care about you. Alongside my family, you are the most important person in the world to me."

She sucked in a breath, her topaz eyes flaring gold, as if she was using her power. He could almost feel it licking inside him, twining with his, wanting to play – but he had to be imagining that because she said she never used her magic; had locked it away.

She licked her lips. "Don't say things you can't possibly mean."

"Why not? I'm allowed to give of my love. I just can't receive it in return." He swallowed against the harsh reality of Eros' curse.

The low rumbling suddenly turned into a roar and the floor bucked under them, sending the shield bubble, and them inside it, up in the air to smash against the roof of the tunnel. "What in all the Hells is going on?" he yelled above the noise as they bounced back to the dirt and rubble-strewn floor.

"As I said, we don't have time for this. We've stayed in one place too long. We've got to move on."

The earth buckled again, sending the bubble bouncing back up the tunnel. He sent out ribbons of power, anchoring it into the wall before they lost more ground. "Is this what you meant when you said things changed down here? Is it because they have earthquakes?"

"Yes but ... this is far more dangerous."

"Why?"

"Don't you get it? We're both alive and corporeal. The Underworld is a place of dead things, not living beings. We're not supposed to be here and it knows it. It's trying to push us back."

"But you live in the palace."

"That's different. It's Hades' private space and he sets the rules there."

"He's the King of the Underworld. Doesn't he set the rules for everything down here?"

She shook her head, hands going out against the edges of his shield to steady herself – her touch was a caress on his magic that almost made him groan. Instead, he leaned in closer to hear her above the noise.

"... not the one who created this place. The old Gods did that – and it is still subject to the basic rules they set. The Living Realms are for the living, the Death Realms are for the dead. Even if you had more time, we would still have to hurry through these tunnels."

"I thought the Hells-Keys were supposed to allow us to slip through easily."

"This *is* easily for a corporeal being."

He shook his head at her. "And you've been down here before?"

"There were souls I needed to interview."

He couldn't help but smiling. "I always liked it when you were a little crazy."

"No time for insults – this will only get worse if we don't keep moving. It can't latch onto our essences as easily if we keep moving."

He let her go, turning to pick up the water bottle he'd dropped on the ground. "I'm glad you're here, given you're knowledge-girl."

She harrumphed at him as she resettled her pack on her back, but her lips were twitching. "Come on, non-knowl-edge-boy."

"That's idiot-boy to you."

Her snort of laughter had delight bubbling in his veins as they jogged forward, his shield protecting them from the ground that continued to rumble and shake around them.

Something had changed between them. It wasn't what it was before, but he was willing to work on it with her to get it back there. She may not be able to love him because of his curse, but life sure was better with her in it, especially if he could help her to forgive herself for whatever she imagined she'd done. He wasn't going to let her disappear from his life ever again.

Whoever or whatever had kept them apart last time wasn't going to succeed again. If they tried that shit again, they'd find out the hard way that this time he'd fight to the death to keep her with him.

CHAPTER
EIGHT

As they jogged, the screams of the inhabitants of the lower chambers became louder and louder. The map indicated the most direct route was through the Morningstar's lands, the entrance to Tartarus currently closest to his kingdom than any other Hell Realm.

The faster they moved, the fewer the quakes around them.

"You get the feeling the Underworld still isn't happy we're here?" he said to Rinna, trying to make her laugh.

She just shot him a look. "Did you really think it was going to be easy?"

"No. Quite frankly, it's same old same old. I've come to expect things to always be difficult." Including, apparently, his relationship with her. At one time, it was one of the easiest things in his life; a blessing he'd never thought to have. Of course he should have expected it to get ripped away. He glanced at her as she jogged, a frown on her face once more. "What is it?"

Her shadowed gaze met his. "Has life really not been easy for you?"

"Why would it have been?"

She shrugged. "I don't know. You always seemed so charmed. Everything came easy to you. And you know … you're a cupid."

"Are you kidding me? I had to fight every day not to be left behind. Everyone was better at everything than me. And there wasn't a group I could truly belong to, not at the training camp and not outside of it." He'd got used over the years to being called a mutt or a mongrel. "But at least at the camp I had you. When Eros took me, I had no one."

"You had Eros."

He snorted. "Eros might be my grandfather but that doesn't mean anything when it comes to the other cupids or the job I had to do. He gave me the training the others get then left me on my own."

"Isn't that what happens to the other cupids?"

"Maybe. But they are made to be cupids – I'm not. Also, they don't have to deal with having both cupid and warlock powers. And they certainly didn't have the Gods and Goddesses interfering constantly; everyone always so interested in the cupid with a demi-God father and a reincarnating-witch mother tied to a curse. It felt like I was constantly under the microscope; everyone expecting me to fail or setting me up to fail."

"Did you?"

He shook his head, jaw firmed. "Not once. I wouldn't give those miserable sods the satisfaction."

"I had no idea."

"Why would you?"

They ran around a curve only to come upon another rockfall. "Damn it!" she said, instantly backing up while glancing at the map again. "That was the last path into the Morningstar's lands." They'd tried a dozen others before

84

being turned around by rockfalls blocking the way or tunnels being cut in two by what looked like bottomless chasms. "Hades is going to be really pissed there's this much damage."

"This can't be the first time this has happened."

She shook her head. "No, but I can't remember it ever being this bad."

"Maybe the portents Persephone mentioned are causing even more havoc than we thought they would."

"Or, maybe the Underworld – or something – doesn't want us to get to Clodia."

He groaned. "Why did you have to say that out loud? Now you've jinxed us."

She narrowed her eyes at him. "I did not jinx us. There is no such thing."

The ground rumbled again, bucking under their feet even though they were moving back up the tunnel. "You think?" he said.

She tried to look at the map as they jogged. "This way," she said, indicating a tunnel she'd chosen not to go down earlier.

It was darker than the tunnel they'd been in, doors lining either side a few metres apart.

A hand shot out between the bars of the cell as Tamuel jogged past. He dodged it. Another hand tried a grab at him from the next cell, its bone-like fingers scraping his shoulder, trying to latch on.

"Watch out," Rinna said, yanking him away. "You don't want to let them touch you."

"Why? What can they do?" He eyed the cell doors and the rickety-looking bars that didn't seem secure at all. From further down, a pathetic wail started, picked up by another soul, and another, until the air was full of wailing.

"Nothing magical," Rinna shouted over the din. "But they can tear at your flesh. And eat it."

"Ew!"

She shrugged. "Well, cupid flesh wouldn't sound so bad if you've not had anything to eat for thousands of years."

He twisted to look at the bony arm still stretched out, reaching for him even though he was too far away. "They've been here for thousands of years?"

"Earthly Realm time. Here it's far longer."

"How can Hades stand having to come down here?"

Korinna bit her lip. "I don't know. He doesn't talk about it and I've never wanted to ask." She'd always suspected it was torture for him, but it was a guess she didn't want confirmed; she hated to think that the God who'd protected and cosseted her and let her hide away in his home for all these years was being tortured by the job he was forced to do.

"No. I suppose I don't really want the answer to that question either," Tam said, echoing her thoughts.

She glanced at him. He frowned into the dark of the tunnel – the narrowest they'd been through so far – eyeing the bars of the cells and the darkness that hid untold torture within.

"Come on, we need to keep moving. But keep to the middle of the tunnel."

"You don't have to tell me twice."

They trudged on, winding their way through the tunnels, keeping to a brisk pace, eating and drinking on the move.

They spoke of many things as they walked over the next few days – or what passed for days in the Underworld. It was often hard to tell given there was no day or night – but somehow, she managed to keep him from asking what he'd started to ask before the first earthquake hit. She knew she couldn't keep his questions at bay forever, but she really didn't want to see the look on his face when he found out – pity or disgust, equally bad – and she certainly didn't want to have the conversation about what she'd vowed.

He didn't need to know she planned to die to fulfil it. That was nobody's business but her own. But she'd never been very good at lying to him. She rounded a corner. Maybe she could tell him the basics to stop him questioning further and—

She almost fell over the edge of a yawning chasm.

Tam's arm slammed out in front of her. "Careful."

"I see it as well as you," she said, shaking her head at him, more annoyed with herself than him. She glanced down at the map. It shouldn't have been there.

"This is ridiculous. We've been walking for two days. You need to rest. You're exhausted."

She glared at him, hating that aside from the few smudges of dirt on his face and the shoulder of his black tunic, he looked as fresh as when they started out. "I don't need a rest."

"Rinna. That is obviously untr—"

She held her hand up. "I don't need you to protect me. I've been looking after myself for almost two thousand years."

"Have you?"

The way his gaze flickered over her made her hyper-aware of the bagginess of her clothes, the shadows under cheeks and eyes, the paleness of her skin.

She bit the inside of her cheek as she backed away from the crumbling edge. "I can't rest even if I wanted to. It's not going to let us. We have to keep going."

He stared at her for a long moment, but when the earth

rumbled below them and more of the edge fell into the chasm, forcing them back, he simply said, "Where to?"

She glanced down at the map – it shifted and changed, changed again, and again before settling, indicating a passage they'd passed half a day ago. It led into a larger chamber, one that had a tunnel leading straight to the Gates of Tartarus. She bit her lip. "Is there another way," she asked the map. It didn't alter.

"What's wrong?"

"Nothing. It should be fine. It's just, I've heard it's one of the worst parts of the Underworld tunnels."

"Worse than what we've been through?"

"Much worse."

He glanced back at the chasm. "We don't really have a choice, do we?"

"No."

The earth beneath them suddenly surged up, tossing them to the ceiling. Tam threw a shield bubble around them again before they hit the roof. He managed to right them as they bounced off the roof and keep them moving back from the chasm that widened with every rumble. The screams of the damned filled the air as one cell after another fell into the bottomless pit.

"Poor bastards."

Korinna nodded – it didn't matter that the souls here had deserved their incarceration and torture – being swallowed by the Underworld wasn't a final death she would wish on anyone.

They bumped up the tunnel, Tam obviously doing everything he could to steady their progress, but they overshot the narrow entrance the map indicated they had to go down, the earth pushing them back and back.

"This is ridiculous," Tam grumbled. "It's like it's trying to kill us now, not get rid of us."

"Who's jinxing us now?"

"It's not a jinx if it's actually happening to—"

She held up her hand as the hairs on the back of her neck stood up and a chill ran over her body. "Shh."

"What?"

She shushed him, listening. Then the sound she'd never wanted to hear again. "Hells, no. What are they doing here?"

"What?"

"Wraiths. Up ahead," she whispered, pointing to the glow that shone from the tunnel she'd planned to go down. Not the reddish-orange glow that lit most of the passages, but a sickly green one that writhed and moved, tentacles of it reaching out as if probing the air, seeking, hunting. The sound that had caught her attention – harsh whispers filled with screams – drew closer.

"Quick, we have to hide."

CHAPTER
NINE

Korinna rushed to the side of the tunnel, relieved to find that the fissure she'd noticed on the way down was still there despite all the earth's movements. In fact, she thought it might have widened a little. They could both squeeze in and hide until the wraiths were past. "Come on," she whispered over her shoulder.

Tam stood where he was in the centre of the tunnel, staring at her. "What are you worried about? Wraiths can't kill us. Not while we're wearing the Hells-Keys."

"Shh," she said, grabbing his arm to pull him into the mouth of the fissure. "They'll hear you."

"Still don't see the problem," he whispered loudly.

Of course he didn't. "They can't kill us down here like they can in the Earthly Realm," she whispered as she pulled him closer, intent on squeezing into the small space. "But they can hurt us. Physically and spiritually."

"Spiritually? I've never heard they could do that."

Damn him for focusing on that part of what she'd said. "Yeah, they pull out your deepest secrets, your darkest emotions, and use them against you. But that's not what

I'm worried about." She was, but she wasn't about to admit that to him. "You think the earthquakes and tremblings have been bad? You don't want to know what will happen if we spill blood down here. Now shut up and hide with me." Her lips were almost against his ear now – she really didn't want the wraiths to hear her. They were busy moaning – the shrieks of the stolen souls inside them coming out of their open maws – but if they stopped, they'd hear her and Tam clearly even if they were hidden by the crevice.

"What are they doing here?" he asked, finally using his inside whisper-voice. "With the veil fading tonight, I would have thought they'd have more auspicious places to be than down here."

"They've still got days, remember? Plenty of time to power up – which they'll need to do if they want to break through the veil and haunt more than these halls. Now shush and get in here. They'll still be able to see you." He nodded and pushed forward, crowding her. "Oof. When did you get so big?"

"Ms Korinna! Such a personal question," he whispered, his lips touching her ear, making her shiver as frissons of electricity rode through her nerves. "But I'm glad you noticed."

She would have smacked him for his teasing in the past – such a cupid thing to do – but she couldn't seem to muster the ability, her entire body revelling in the sensation of his warm strength pushing up against her.

He pushed closer. Her back hit rock.

"Am I in?"

She ignored the sexually tinged words whispered against her ear and glanced over his shoulder to the nasty green glow lighting up the tunnel beyond. The lips of the crevice were just beyond his back. He really was very broad-shouldered. "No. The fissure isn't deep enough for its shadows to hide you from the wraiths' glow."

If only she could take a chance and use her magic to protect him, but she couldn't risk it getting out of her control once again. Couldn't risk another mistake of judgement. Couldn't risk another person she cared for being killed. But then magic tingled in the air around them; a cloud of darkness starting to cover the entrance behind him. He was trying to protect them, but she wasn't sure it was going to be enough.

She opened her mouth to tell him he'd need to change his spell, but her jaw snapped shut as the wraiths' ugly magic whispered along the walls, calling to her. Whispering voices urging her to unburden herself of every hidden thing inside her.

She firmed her mind's shields against them but it wasn't quite enough. Memories she never let in, except in nightmares, flooded into her mind: the volcanic rumblings; the ruling council of Pompeii coming to her, worried, seeking help; her calming response that made them ignore what was so obvious – that she didn't have control over the sleeping volcanic God, Vesuvius, in the way she should. Instead of evacuating, they went about their business, trusting her; trusting her judgement.

That moment looped in her mind now as it did in her nightmares. So stupid and prideful to think she could handle it alone, that she didn't need to call Seph or Demeter for instructions on what to do. She'd been so hurt by Tam's leaving, his betrayal, that she was determined to prove she could do this without him or anyone.

She couldn't stop the images from playing out; when she'd headed out from her temple, past the still-worried people, soothing their fear with waves of her magic, a stupid, beneficent smile on her face; she'd felt so pleased with herself as she'd left them behind, laughing and smiling and shouting after her their love and worship as they must have done for her mother when she was their Guardian, and headed up the volcano to soothe Vesuvius, to bind him with a spell of restful sleeping. But her magic faltered and instead of soothing Vesuvius into a peaceful, dreamless sleep, she woke him up. Her magic had worked fine as she'd transported herself back to Pompeii, her plan to get the people to evacuate. But even as the volcano belched more and more sulphuric clouds into the sky and the ground rumbled and cracked, the people went about their business, still somehow affected by her spell of calm even after she withdrew it.

Then before she could think what to do, the volcano erupted in a gush of fire and clouds of steam and poisonous gas. Her spell of calm finally broke, panic and confusion and terror tearing free. But as it did, she remembered a spell, one she'd read in a book that Tam had smuggled from the camp's library – one they shouldn't have had access to.

As the people started to run – too late. Far too late – and the deadly pyroclastic cloud swept towards them, she didn't give a thought to if she could do such a powerful spell designed for two or more spellweavers; only the words Tam had whispered to her as she'd read the spell that first time – "You could do this. You're powerful enough to do this alone." He'd been so sure, had made her so sure in that moment of panic that she could save the people of Pompeii despite all the signs telling her it was a Fated event.

She attempted to fold space, to transport the entire city and its people elsewhere. But the greatest magic couldn't fight Fate and the spell snapped back at her, the people of Pompeii paying for her hubris. Instead of transporting them and their city, it cut their souls from their bodies in one, horrifying instant and thrust them through the tear in space she'd created, sucking them instead into the Void that she'd accidentally ripped open with powers that were stronger than a witch should ever have.

They hadn't been killed by the pyroclastic cloud of super-heated dust that enveloped the city a moment later as was told by historians. They'd been killed by her.

They should have all gone to Elysium. Instead, she'd thought to vanquish destiny and had instead forced on them a worse Fate than the one designed for them.

She'd thrown herself forward, screaming her pain, her guilt, her loss, willing to join those souls lost in the Void ... and collided with the shield that sprang up around the temple, protecting it and her from the force of the volcanic explosion.

Even after the tear had snapped closed, her powers flamed out, she continued to throw herself against the shield until her arms and legs and body were bloody and bruised, her voice nothing but ragged gasps, the image of Pompeii as it was swallowed in the volcanic cloud imprinted on her mind for all eternity. She barely noticed Persephone and Demeter arrive until they picked her up and carried her away. She tried to stop them, to stay, to undo what had been done, but they were implacable and she was too weak in every way to fight them, the spell having drained everything from her except her life. She wished it had finished its job.

That feeling of helplessness, of being wrong, of choosing wrongly, had never left her. It pulled at her even now as the wraiths writhed their way forward, urging her to give up on a quest she was unlikely ever to finish. She wasn't strong enough. The Fates weaving of their threads might have made her spellwork falter but they hadn't affected her reason. She'd been prideful and selfish in thinking she could change what was meant to happen. She was a screw up. Why did she think she could make it right? Hadn't she learned she couldn't trust her decisions? Couldn't trust her instincts? She really should give up. Should just go out there and let the wraiths have her pain, her guilt, her secret.

Not that it was truly a secret. Persephone, Hades, Demeter – they all knew what had happened; what she'd done. It didn't matter that they'd spent centuries trying to make her believe that she could have done nothing to stop the deaths and that what happened wasn't her fault. She knew those platitudes for what they were – the desperate words of people who didn't want to face that what had happened to the people of Pompeii ultimately *was* her fault. They might have been Fated to die but *she* was the reason their souls were lost in the Void, in eternal pain, rather than enjoying the bliss of Elysium, as had been their Fate.

She was responsible for that horror. An eternal horror. Unless she fixed it. But could she fix it? Maybe giving in to the wraiths' fatal call was her penance. That her soul deserved to be as lost as the Pompeiians were.

"Rinna, by all the Hells. I can't believe ... What are you doing?"

She looked at her hands pressed against his chest. He was in her way. "I need to get out there."

"Why?"

She looked up at him. "They're calling to me. Can't you hear them? I need to go to them. They'll take it all. Everything I've done. They'll make me pay. Truly pay. I have to go. Let me go."

She pushed him, but he was a rock, immovable, his arms tight around her.

"No, Rinna. Don't listen to them. It wasn't your fault. What happened wasn't your fault."

"You know?" She gasped as her gaze met his; at the shadows of her grief and pain reflected there.

But then they were gone as quickly as they'd come and he said, "About Pompeii? Everyone knows the volcanic explosion was Fated. You couldn't have saved those people."

"I know that!" She wanted her voice to be a yell, but it came out as a harsh, pain-filled whisper. "But their souls. I lost their souls. And I have to get them back. It's my penance. At least, I thought it was. But maybe my true penance is giving up my soul." Her gaze slid to the green glow over his shoulder seen even through his shadow-cloak hanging in the crevice opening. She pushed against him again. Maybe she should use her magic against him.

"Rinna." His voice, a harsh explosion of air against her face as he shook her. "Look at me, Rinna."

She didn't want to, but something in his voice reached inside her, forcing her gaze to his.

"Don't give into them. Whatever pain they're calling to, don't give in to it. If you do, you will never be able to set right whatever it is you think you did. And you want that, don't you? To set it right?"

Yes. Yes, she did. With everything in her. She nodded.

"Then fight it. Fight the compulsion."

"I can't," she said, the wraiths' call barbed tendrils in her mind. "I'm too weak. Always too weak. I missed the signs telling me I was supposed to let them go, to shepherd their souls to Elysium as they deserved. I thought I could fix it, but I just made it so much worse. I deserve everything bad coming to me."

"No." His arms tightened around her, his gaze a black blaze – he was using his warlock powers, building a shield bubble around them – why hadn't he done that before? – pulling the shadow-cloak around it, the sensation shivering over her like a caress. She should wonder why that was, but the ebony of his eyes captured her and all she could think of was him. There was nothing but black in his eyes now. It should have terrified but instead it fascinated her as it always had. This sign, of him using his warlock powers, had confused all their trainers and teachers; was something they'd never been able to train out of him. Why they'd ever want to, she didn't know – his black eyes were as beautiful and magnetic as the indigo gifted to him from his cupid heritage.

The shadow-shield he created pulled in around them. It should have been cold and frightening, but as it always had been, Tam's magic was a warm fur blanket brushing against her skin. His power – so achingly familiar – shivered over her, through her, its touch a caress, bringing light where there was darkness; hope where there was doubt; prying loose the wraiths' barbed tendrils, turning them to dust.

And as the tendrils disintegrated, Tam's words, a faint echo to begin with, grew louder, filling up her mind, pushing out the images that haunted her in her sleep, that had come to her with the wraiths' call, replacing them with a single image: her nestled in the safety and warmth of his arms, protected, loved.

Even though she knew it couldn't be true, that she didn't deserve it, she clung to it; it protected her as much as his shield did from the wraiths' compulsive call.

The shrieking came closer, the sickening glow lighting up the tunnel over Tam's shoulder – his power allowing her to see through the cloud even though she could no longer feel the pull of the wraiths. So clever, her cupid. One of them needed to see when the danger had passed; he had gifted that control to her.

Wraith tendrils writhed along the opposite wall, more tendrils appearing around the edges of the fissure, probing the shadow-shield.

She gripped Tam tightly – when had she stopped pushing at him and put her arms around him? – and pulled him even closer, his body a rigid wall in front of her, protecting her.

But what was protecting him? Was his shadow-shield strong enough to protect him from the wraiths' seeking tendrils?

The shadow darkened, but she could still see through it. The wraiths appeared, their forms constantly shifting, flickering between shapes and faces – all the souls they'd devoured. Their mouths were open, their horrifying, wailing song a warning. But like a siren's song, it called spirits to them even as it terrified.

Souls that had been freed from their cells by the earthquakes, but somehow hadn't fallen into the chasm, rushed up the tunnel, throwing themselves into the wraiths' embrace. Of course, one touch and they were gone – their screams adding to the wraiths' terrible song.

She shuddered. If not for Tam, that would have been her. If she'd gone to them, she would have failed. She couldn't fail. She couldn't.

Tam's arms tightened around her. Comfort? No. He trembled. Did he feel the wraiths' call sliding along his shield, and sought comfort from her? Or maybe protection?

A foolish notion – someone as powerful as he didn't need protection from one such as she. And yet, he held her so tightly, trembling, his gaze never leaving hers as if seeking her strength, her support. What did he feel? What demons did he fight as the wraiths' tendrils slid over his shields? She wished she knew. Wished she could help him fight them. But she couldn't trust the choices she made with her magic.

So, she held on tightly, her fingers finding their way under his black top to his skin, pressing tightly, holding onto him as he held onto her.

They stayed like that until the wraiths' moans had disappeared in the distance – the widening chasm wouldn't have stopped their journey at all, especially fuelled by new souls as they were.

She relaxed a little, but for some reason, didn't let go of Tam as he let go of his spell. The darkness that had hidden them from the wraiths' glow slipped away.

"That was fun," he said softly, his breath moving over her face, their eyes still locked together.

"Fun?" she whispered.

His mouth quirked in the corner and she lost her breath. He was so handsome, his eyes indigo once again, his skin glowing a little from the power he'd unleashed. His smile widened as he looked at her, that little flicker at the corners of his lips and eyes that made things flutter in her stomach. "Maybe not fun. But at least the Underworld's stopped trying to kill us."

"Yes," she managed, her attention caught by the smudge of dirt on his brow. She reached up without thinking to rub it away, but her fingers caught in the softness of the hair that had fallen over his brow as he looked down at her.

"Rinna," he said, brushing her hair back from her face, his large palms cupping her cheeks. "You okay?"

She'd been dreading those words. She didn't want to talk about it – she'd already said far too much. So she just said, "I'm fine. Thanks for ... that." She waved her hand to encompass the space behind him.

"You never have to thank me for helping you. I only wish I could have been there for you all those years ago. Maybe if I had, things wouldn't have gotten this bad for you."

She swallowed hard. She wanted to tell him not to waste his time or energy on saving her – she couldn't be saved – but instead, all that came out was, "We should get going."

"We should."

He didn't move. Not surprising given she still gripped him tightly, her fingers kneading warm skin. Their bodies pressed closer. He cupped her face. Her hands slid up his back and around to his chest, flexing against muscle and hot-hot skin.

He was broader across the chest and shoulders than she remembered, his muscles well defined. And standing like this, she realised he was taller now; over six feet by a couple of inches at least, enough that he had half a head on her, making her look up at him. She'd always hated having to look up to anyone, but with him ... she didn't mind at all.

"Rinna," he said harshly. "If you don't stop, we're soon going to discover just how big I can get."

She licked her suddenly dry lips. "I don't see the problem." After what she'd just been through, she was desperate to feel something of life, of living; and the pull of him, the pleasant burn of his skin against hers was certainly that. It had always been like this with him. Right from the first

100

moment she'd seen him; the teenager demi-God-cupid who should have hung with the warrior boys he was supposed to train with, but instead, when asked who he wanted as his training partner, had pointed at her. He'd won her friendship in that moment and her heart not long after.

She'd been so stupid to think he would have left her of his own free will with no word for all these centuries. He was her friend. Her best friend. As she'd been his. She hadn't doubted it back then when they'd been together. Why had she so easily doubted it after he left?

She wished she could take the time to find out who had got in between them and why. But once his quest was finished, he would go and she would have what she needed to finish hers. Whoever had got between them, whoever had wanted them to stay apart, would get their way.

Because no matter how much she loved Tamuel, it didn't matter. They had no future. Not simply because she no longer deserved to be loved.

She had made a vow and there was no backing out of it. No choice.

There was only choice in *this*. Only choice in the *now*.

And she chose to show Tam just how much she loved him. If not in words, then with her body and soul, giving all she was to him in *this* moment.

A moment she would carry with her, giving her strength until the very end.

She might not be able to trust her magical choices; might not be able to trust herself. But she could trust him. She always had. "I trust you, Tam. I want this."

Light flashed in his eyes, his fingers shifting in her hair. His gaze probed hers for long, breathless seconds.

She reached up, grabbed his head and brought it down to hers, taking his lips in an open-mouthed kiss, all tongue and teeth. He opened beneath her onslaught, the flavour of him – the tartness of red wine mixed with the sweetness of berries – filling her mouth.

She moaned. Kissing him felt better than she'd ever imagined – and she'd imagined a lot.

She was kissing her Tam.

No, not her Tam. This was a new Tam. A Tam who had grown into a sexy, handsome, powerful male, one who'd lived a life; who might not have guilt or regret, but had known pain. His pain resonated alongside hers, different but somehow the same. Why could she feel it like she did? There was no answer to be had right now, nor did she want one.

All she could think about was getting closer. She was sick of fighting it. Tired of going without what she wanted; what she needed.

Skin. She needed to feel skin.

She pushed his long coat away from his shoulders, pulled at his tunic, at the ties securing it closed. His hands were busy too. Air brushed her skin a split second before her fingers splayed over his naked chest.

"Rinna," he said, the sound desperate. A plea. "Not here. Not like this."

She wanted to answer his plea. He was right.

But sense didn't enter into the passion driving through her that she could no longer ignore; the edginess of her desire was akin to skating on the edge of sanity. She had to give in to it. To set herself free for just this moment. It might be her last chance to ever feel like this.

So instead of roping herself in as she knew she should, she let go.

CHAPTER
TEN

Tamuel resisted, his fingers tightening on her face, trying his best to pull her away. "Please, Rinna," he said against her mouth. "Not like this."

She reared back. "Exactly like this."

"We need to talk about what happened with the wraiths."

"Later." She slipped a hand to the back of his head, fingers twining in the silk of his hair, holding him to her as she ran her other hand over the delicious planes of his chest, his shoulders, his back.

He sucked in a breath. "Fine. But it's not safe and ..." He moaned as she licked his lips. "You deserve more," he choked out.

"No. I don't." She gripped his face. The place and time didn't matter. All that mattered was that she wanted him. Loved him. Always. She hadn't wanted to admit that love had stayed with her because it hurt too much; because she'd held onto her mad over the fact he'd left, even though she'd known – had *known* – he'd had no choice. She could admit that now. Just as she could admit to herself that she wanted him. And that this would be her last chance to do something about it. "The roof could come down around us and I wouldn't care."

"I would. I don't want you hurt."

"Protect us with your bubble then, because unless you tell me you don't want me, don't want this, it's happening."

His hands were suddenly in her hair, his thumbs brushing over her cheeks. "I want you more than I've ever wanted anything. But after. When I have time to worship you properly."

She shook her head, tears pricking her eyes, her throat thick. "No. Now. I need this now." Her fingers tightened in his hair. "Don't make me beg," she whispered.

"But the Underworld — won't it object that we've stopped in one place? The roof might quite literally come down on our heads."

"I trust you to shield us." She bit her lip.

His gaze dipped to it. "I hate it when you do that."

"Then stop me."

His eyes glowed, then his lips came down on hers and she was lost.

The earth bucked around them, widening the fissure, the rock behind her crumbling to the floor. She fell backwards, her arms tight around Tamuel, taking him with her.

She landed on a soft cushion of air, his shield a bubble around them, deflecting the spray of dirt and rubble coming down from the rocks above as the earth buckled and warped around them, trying to push them back. But the bubble was caught in the fissure and so were they.

"Clever cupid," she said as she broke from his kiss, her fingers gripped tight in his silky auburn hair.

"I try." His lips curled into the grin that seemed to tap into something deep inside her, pulling on strings of desire that ricocheted through her, bringing fire in their wake.

She pulled his head back down so she could suck on his lower lip before tangling her tongue with his. His hands ran over her, cupping her naked breast – where had her undergarments gone? – the gem he wore around his neck warm where it touched her skin. He tore his mouth from hers – she whimpered her protest – but then blazed fire down her throat, across her chest to her nipple.

Ye Gods!

He ran his tongue around the taught peak before sucking it into his mouth, his other hand moving down her stomach, tickling through her curls and sliding into the wet heat hidden there.

"Hmm," he mumbled against her breast, the vibration of sound adding to the incredible sensation of his tongue on her skin. "Ready already?"

"I've been ready for a long time."

He raised his head, gaze grabbing at hers. No humour flashed in his eyes, just need and a longing so old she felt it in her soul. He held her gaze and moved his fingers across the sensitive nub between her legs, sliding his thumb inside her aching core.

She trembled. He repeated the movement, over and over while he watched her, his gaze glued to her face.

The trembling started small, deep inside her, but then expanded, radiating out, until she was nothing but the tremble and a hot rushing sensation she didn't want to come to completion. Not yet.

"Cum for me, Rinna. Let go."

"Not without you."

She grabbed for him – he still had his pants on. Damn. But almost like magic, the buttons and ties of the leather pants he wore that matched hers – like the ones they'd worn in training all those years ago; all the better to kick-arse in – came undone with barely a touch and they fell down his legs.

"Slow down," he said, as if shocked to lose his pants so quickly when she knew it was his magic that had helped her.

"Naughty cupid," she whispered against his lips as she took the full length of him in her hands. He hissed against her lips, the sound feeding her desire, bringing her pleasure like she'd never known. She'd held a man's cock in her hands before, but it had never been like holding his. Thick and long, hot and silken, it twitched as she stroked it.

"Keep that up and I'll never make it inside you."

She smiled against his lips. She was tempted to bring him to completion with just her hand on his cock and her tongue in his mouth, but …

She wanted more. So much more. She wanted everything she could have in this bubble of time.

The earth below them groaned, the walls shook; the fissure opened wider, trying to push them out, to force them back where they belonged.

The bubble expanded, wedging them in tight. She expected the cushioning sensation that held her to loosen with its expansion, but it didn't – it still felt like she was lying on the softest down-filled bed.

Her cupid. Looking after her. As she always knew he would.

Keeping her gaze on his, she guided him to her centre. His hand had found her breast again, squeezed as she changed their positions so she was on top. Slowly, so slowly, she lowered herself onto the long, thick length of him.

She wanted to close her eyes to savour the feeling of him deep inside her, sliding deeper, but she didn't want to stop watching him. His face, it was an artist's rendering, an angel succumbing to earthly pleasure and she wanted to take in her fill.

"Rinna," he breathed – she loved the sound of her name on his lips. "By the Gods." His other hand gripped her hip as he filled her entirely in all the right ways.

He flexed his hips, edging up into her further – she didn't think it was possible. Pleasure shivered through her, a quake to match the shaking of the earth all around them. She arched backwards, one hand sweeping down his chest to his abdomen, the other reaching up to cover the hand on her breast. His fingers, so long and fine, strong but gentle, teasing her flesh.

"Gods, you are beautiful, my Rinna."

Her gaze slammed back to his. Nobody had ever called her beautiful before. She knew she wasn't. She was pleasant to look at, but her features were a little too off-kilter to ever be called beautiful – her eyes a little too large; her lips a little too wide; her chin a little too pointed – but in his eyes, she saw that she was. Beautiful. Goddess-like.

He said he wanted to wait so he could worship her properly, but she had no idea how he could worship her more than he did right now. It couldn't ever get better than this. Except ...

She began to move. He joined her, his hips flexing, his cock sliding in and out of her in just the right way, making all her nerve endings sing. She wanted to hold his gaze, to watch the pleasure mount on his face, but she also wanted his lips back on hers.

She leaned down, her breasts brushing over the planes of his chest, hands in his hair, tasting, sucking, tongues and teeth and breath mingled.

One.

They were one.

He rose up, arms going around her as he slammed in even deeper, just how she needed him to without even knowing she did. He held her face close to his, breath a harsh pant, brushing over her skin, moving her hair, his gaze meshed with hers as he moved deep inside her, the passion-laden hunger notching up and up.

"I want you, Rinna. I love you. I always have."

She gasped, pleasure dipping for a moment as his words hit. Undeserved. Besides, he was probably just lost in the moment. Men could say all sorts of things when they were balls deep inside a woman – or so the other Soteira had said to her.

Yet, she longed to return his words; but she couldn't do that to him. So she said, "I need you, Tam. I always have," and hoped it would be enough to carry him through any dark times ahead. She wanted him to remember this moment and smile, not grieve over a lost love that could never be theirs.

His eyes glowed at her words, the shield around them taking on the amethyst hue of his cupid powers sparking deep inside their hidden depths. A golden glow flickered alongside the blue, strengthening them – something new in his warlock powers? – then he moved faster. And faster.

His lips slammed back down on hers, his taste inside her, his scent covering her, claiming her. One hand held her hips while he stroked her breasts with the other. The sensation inside her squeezed tighter and tighter. He moved his hand down her stomach, his thumb slipping into the wet heat of her, finding the nub that was the heart of her pleasure. He pressed, once, twice, three times, pounding and pounding inside her as his tongue played with hers and ...

"Tamuel!" she gasped, breath sawing in her lungs, her throat, as fire sparked in her nerves, becoming a blaze, exploding out, lifting her up and tossing her higher and higher, lit everywhere by the glow – golden and amethyst and blue melded together.

His cry lit the air a moment later as he pulsed around her, inside her.

For a timeless moment, all she was aware of was him and her, their hands holding tight, the warm dampness of their skin sliding against each other as the pleasure trembled through them, his lips on hers as he whispered words of love, as if to breathe the life of them inside her. As if they were true. As if she deserved them.

She opened her eyes. Chaos reigned outside the shield, but she didn't care. Not when his head was buried between her breasts, his breath and silky hair brushing her skin in a delightful way she wished she had time to explore. She ran her hand up his back, into his hair – slightly damp. So was hers. She could feel it sticking to her forehead, her neck. "That was quite the workout," she said softly.

He chuckled, the sound vibrating through her. Ye Gods, she loved that feeling, wanted more.

But the Underworld had other plans.

The earth around them shook even more violently. The fissure widened. The shield trembled under the barrage of rocks raining down on it, but stayed strong – he was so powerful. To have kept the shield's strength up like he had while losing himself to pleasure with her ... remarkable.

As the earth bucked and trembled around them, Tam

finally lifted his head, his mouth twisted in a wicked grin. "Did I just make the earth move for you or what?"

She laughed. She couldn't help it.

Then the earth spit the bubble out of the fissure and they were falling, falling, down through the crevice that had widened up the tunnel to swallow them whole.

CHAPTER

ELEVEN

T amuel shifted, wrapping Rinna in his arms, throwing everything he had into the shield as they fell.

The world shrieked around them, spirits flying in a tornado-type whorl with them in the centre. He looked down, below the bubble, but could see nothing but darkness.

Fucking Hells! What had he done?

He'd been stupid and reckless to give in to her demands. She was just reacting to the fact they were in danger. To the memories she'd somehow shared with him when the wraiths passed them. By all that was holy, what she had been through! Why had the Gods sent her to that post knowing she must fail? Why had they not told her? There was so much to delve into, so much to find answers for so that she might finally find some peace, and he'd meant to but then she'd kissed him and touched him and told him she needed him, and he'd been too weak to fight the need that always simmered below the surface for her. Only her.

But he should have done better. Been better.

111

Eternal bloody hells. He'd told her he loved her. What a gauche idiot. It wasn't like she could say it back. Nobody could love him. It was part of his curse.

He was the one who should be in danger, not her.

Well, he might have been a weak idiot, but he wasn't a powerless one.

The Underworld might not be happy they were trying to travel through it, but it wasn't going to force them back and he'd be damned if he would let it kill them. Hades had given him permission to be here and he was going to force it to see reason.

"Stop!" he yelled, his voice booming out of the shield as he roped in the magic inside him, utilising both his cupid and warlock magics, even though the two most often did not work side by side very well and his warlock magic was largely untrained. But right now, both sides of his magic were stronger than he'd ever felt them. Maybe they were still being boosted by the power he'd borrowed from his family's hidden vault? Although, that hadn't felt anything like this.

This ... it was glorious. Like he'd always been missing something and was now suddenly being made whole. Whatever it was, his use of all of what he had worked.

The spirits scattered.

The rocks stopped falling.

The shield bounced to a stop.

Everything fell silent.

Except for Rinna's gasp of breath against his ear.

She clung to him, her nails digging into his skin. She must be scared shitless.

Holding onto her, he guided the glowing blue, amethyst and golden bubble safely to the ground, noticing it now had little flecks of deep red flickering along its surface as well.

He had no idea where the red, gold and blue had come from – maybe the Underworld had changed his powers. He'd ask Rinna, after they were safe. And after all the other things he needed to ask her.

He used his powers to clothe them and, with the earth finally silent and still, let go of the shield.

She didn't let him go, her body pressed tight against his. "You can let go now," he said softly. "It's safe."

She held onto him as she looked up – was she still frightened? "How did you do that?"

He shrugged. "I was going to ask you if you knew. My powers feel and look different here. I thought maybe the Underworld had affected them in some way."

She frowned. "I've never heard of that before but I guess it's possible. There's not been many living people with powers down here to test the theory. I wonder if Hades would let me have a control group ..." Her words faded, frown deepening, then she shook her head. "None of that matters right now." She met his gaze. "Can you use your powers to get us closer to Tartarus?"

He shook his head. "I don't think so. Although, I don't think there's a need." He pointed behind her.

She turned slowly, not letting go of him – he was sorry she'd been frightened so badly. Although, now he thought about it, she didn't seem to be clinging to him in fright. He looked down at her. She smiled as his gaze met hers, touched his lips with her fingertips, rubbed her body against his. "If we have time, I look forward to you moving my world like that again."

Bloody Hells.

Joy sparked through him, filling his chest. Could he smile any wider? "Gladly." She might not be able to return his love, but there was no doubt she wanted him. It was something at least. "It's not like me to look a gift horse in the mouth."

"I'm a gift horse?"

He brushed his thumb over the crease of her frown. "The best gift with nary a horse in sight."

She laughed softly. "You're so silly." She leaned up and kissed him. "I'm glad you're my silly cupid. For now." Sadness filled her eyes for a second, but then she looked away, gesturing to the gate at the end of the tunnel. "Speaking of gift horses ..."

"I know. Lucky, right?"

She shrugged. "Maybe. Or maybe the Underworld listened to you back there after all and decided the best way to get rid of us was to let us get here faster."

"Maybe. At least it's not trying to kill us anymore."

"It doesn't have to. Not when we are going in there."

He turned her to face him. "You don't have to come. In fact, don't come. I shouldn't have asked you to help me with this. I don't want you to get hurt."

She shook her head, the glow of something wild and reckless in her eyes that he'd never seen in her before. "I'm not backing out now. Not when we're so close. Besides, you have no choice. Clodia won't just tell you where she put your mother's powers. The only way is to use the HeartsBlood Gem and it won't work without my help. So, no more trying to coddle and protect me — let's go."

"When did you become so stubborn?"

"A long time ago," she said, eyes shadowed.

He knew he should ask her about the memories he'd seen, but now wasn't the time.

He held out his hand. She took it, then strode towards the towering gates made of bones so old they were black and shiny, glowing in the semi-dark in a way that made his skin crawl.

Korinna couldn't believe what she'd done. Or how keen she was to have it repeated. With him. Only him.

By all the hells. She'd never realised what making love could truly be like – although she suspected it would only ever be like that with him. Her Tamuel. Her best friend. Her forever love.

She wished things could be different, that they hadn't lost all those years, that—

Her thoughts came to a screeching halt as they drew closer to the gate, her mind filled with the screaming that emanated from the black bones it was constructed from; bones that were a warning as much as a method of trapping prisoners.

The Gates of Tartarus. Worse than the Gates of Hell. The entry into a world of nightmares more horrible by a thousand than the one they'd just passed through. For in this place, Titans and the souls of creatures of terrible power were kept to be tortured for eternity. Most of them deserved it. Some were prisoners simply for getting on a God or Goddess' bad side. None could leave. Ever. There was no penance good enough to allow their souls a moment of peace.

The gates sang to her, the song an ache in her bones, her nerves, making her tremble. Similar to the wraiths' song, but instead of making her want to throw herself at them, they pushed at her to stop, to turn back, to run as far and fast as she could. Even with the Hells-Key sunk into the flesh of her chest, she wanted to run screaming in the opposite direction. Hades must have shielded her from the worst of it the few times she'd come here with him, because she'd never felt anything like this before.

Or maybe she'd been changed by the wraiths. She'd pushed those memories down for so long, but now they were at the surface and she was terrified of truly facing them again.

Tamuel clasped her hand tighter in his. She eyed him – he was pale but otherwise didn't show that he was feeling anything close to the terror firing through her veins. He glanced at her. Smiled. Gripped her hand tighter. "Here we go," he said.

She couldn't find her voice so she simply nodded.

They kept going. The gates didn't open. Would the Hells-Key work without Hades as escort? He'd let them come down here by themselves, so it should, but doubt dragged at her like a wet cloak pulling her into the dark of the ocean's depths.

They reached the gates. Tamuel kept walking, never letting go of her. He became transparent for a moment, passing through the gates successfully, his grip pulling her forward. She glanced down. She'd become transparent too. Then her hand passed through the gate.

Cold. So cold. The gates tried to grab at her, gripping her arm, her hair, her legs as she tried to follow Tamuel. It was harder, so much harder, to get through these gates than it ever had been. Her griefs, her torment, rising to sweep her away.

She gasped. She couldn't fight it. She'd be trapped in here forever as she deserved.

"Rinna. Let go. It wasn't your fault."

Tam's words echoed around her. She looked up. She could see him. He still held her hand, his gaze firm on her, full of belief in what he said; belief in her.

She had to do this. For him. For those lost souls. She couldn't fail now. Not when she was so close.

The pressure increased, slowing her passage, squeezing. Painful. She gasped, closing her eyes, pushing forward harder, trying not to panic. She had to get through. Had to. She couldn't get stuck here. Couldn't die here.

"You can do it, my love."

She opened her eyes, caught in Tam's gaze and knew what to do: there was strength in love even when it was undeserved.

She bore down, shoving the ever-present guilt and grief behind the wall of pleasure she'd experienced in Tam's arms only minutes ago. Filled herself with it; with the brilliant joy of him. She remembered every kiss, every touch, every desire-laden pleasure he'd wrought on her body to answer her craving, her hunger.

Let me through. Let me through.

It had to work.

A gasp was squeezed from her as the pressure increased. She grasped at the memory of him looking into her eyes and telling her he loved her.

With a pop, she staggered free, smacking into him, knocking him off his feet.

He instantly sprang up, hands out to catch her, but she was steady as a rock as she looked at him. "Glad to see I can knock you off your feet."

He smiled – ye Gods, that smile – and, "You can knock me off my feet any time, Rinna."

She looked up at him and ...

Laughed.

He laughed with her. The sound rang around them before being swallowed by the red-tinged dark and the screams that lived in the cavern walls.

They fell silent.

The shriek of the chronometer on his wrist broke the

silence. The sound echoed dimly in the cavernous, dampening dark. She shivered as the tinny voice of the chronometer sounded, barely audible above the screams coming from the tunnels ahead.

"The veil is almost completed its thinning. Alignment adjusting ... computing, computing ... The Underworld's position has changed. Time has shifted. One day in the Underworld is now equal to half an hour in the Earthly Realm. The clocks will strike twelve on All Hallows' Eve in two days Tartarus time. Allotted time lost since last computation: four days. Alignment still changing. Further alarms will be forthcoming."

Korinna gripped his arm, staring at the chronometer. "It can't be right."

He looked grim as he shook his head. "It is right. Your design is perfect."

"But you only have two days to complete your task and return to point of origin before the spell expires. It's taken us more than two days to get this far; add to that whatever time it takes to get to Clodia—"

"Then we better hurry." He flashed her a cheeky smile. "Especially given I haven't yet gone into my memory vault to remember the spell to return."

"You didn't memorise the spell?"

He grimaced as he held up his scarred arm. "I didn't think I'd need to; and not all of us have an eidetic memory."

"How will we have time to get you back to Hades' Palace let alone find a quiet space for you to enter your memory vault? If I remember correctly, it always took you hours to navigate your mind's pathways."

"I've improved since then. It shouldn't take more than an hour."

"I see your mathematics hasn't improved. An hour on top of time we already don't have is still an hour too much!"

He shrugged, a mischievous look on his face. "I expect the Underworld will help there. I don't think it will take anywhere near as long to get back as it took to get down here."

She nodded. He was probably right. Even so, it wasn't good news. They had no idea how quickly they could get to Clodia. And while she was certain of the spell to allow him to use the HeartsBlood Gem to force Clodia to tell him what he needed, she had no idea how quickly it would work. Or if it would work for him if she didn't use her magic. So much could go wrong.

"It will be fine," he said, giving her hand a squeeze. "I'm pretty sure I'll be able to change a small part of the Eleusinian Mysteries spell to allow me to portal back from Clodia's cell." He glanced down at the damaged design on his wrist, frowned, muttered, "I think if I change the stroke here and put it there—"

"You think? You don't know?"

He shrugged. "I wasn't expecting Hades to break my arm and Persephone to damage the mark when she healed me."

"Well, he wouldn't want you parading down here with that."

"Yeah, I know. But I didn't intend to bump into him."

She shook her head at him. "You'll get trapped down here if you don't remember it right."

"I know."

She gripped his arm. "Not just trapped. You'll be a prisoner."

"I know. But the risk is worth it." He rubbed his thumb over her frown. "Hey, it will be fine. You know my mind is a steel trap. I've just got to get inside it. Besides, I have you here to help. Nobody was better at ancient spell work than you. I know you'll be able to tell if I do the mark wrong."

"I may not be able to without my magic."

He cupped her face, kissed her softly. "I believe in you."

And he did. It was so clear in his eyes, his trust. And something more. Could it really be love? No. She couldn't let that false hope in. But even so, his belief, his trust, it was bliss. She touched his cheek, wanting to give back some of what he'd given to her. "And I believe in you."

He kissed her again, a smile playing on his lips, but before she could lose herself to the madness of him again, he pulled back. "After."

She only nodded even though she knew there would be no 'after'. He would go back to his home and she would—

"Which way?" he asked.

She suddenly realised she had no idea where the map had gone. She'd dropped it when she'd grabbed him and kissed him earlier. He chuckled, then clicked his fingers, the map landing in her hand. She met his gaze. Even the dark angry terror of this place couldn't dampen the light in his eyes; it gave her the courage to smile and open the map. After finding where they were and where Clodia's cell was situated – closer than she'd ever dared hope – she pointed at a darker space in the wall closest to them. "This way."

Their footsteps were silent, swallowed by the walls and their screams.

CHAPTER
TWELVE

Tartarus didn't seem to object to their presence like the rest of the Underworld did. In fact, beyond the dim light that surged from side passages, flickering from red to green to blue to yellow then back to red, beyond the screams that rose as if from the rocks and soil, there was a pull here. A gripping; as if, rather than wanting them to go, Tartarus longed for them to stay. It had never been like this when she'd come to speak to prisoners with Hades as her guide. But then, his presence was enough to drown out anything else. At least, after what happened to her with the wraiths, she hoped that's what it was.

Close to the entrance cavern, they passed a passage; a sickly yellow light crept out of it across the floor. Voices whispered in the dark, enticing her into the light. Tam's hand tightened on hers as they edged past, his expression grim, his attention focused on the tunnels ahead. Somehow it made her feel better that she wasn't the only one affected.

Half a day's walk brought them to the point the map indicated was the entrance to Clodia's cell. Shrieking echoed out of the red-lit cave, agonised and rage-filled.

Korinna swallowed hard. Zeus and Hades must have been truly pissed with the ancient witch-priestess. But then, as far as they were concerned, the sin of hubris really was the worst.

"Shall we go in?" Tam glanced down at the chronometer.

"Have we lost time?"

"It's still the same as before. We've got time if you want to take a moment before we go in."

She shook her head – even if they had all the time in the Realms, she didn't want to linger any longer than absolutely necessary. "I'm fine." But still, she hesitated; those shrieks coming from the cell rode her nerves, scraping at her skin. If not for Demeter and Seph, this was where she should have ended up; perhaps one day soon, it would be.

Tam touched her cheek. She tore her gaze from the nasty red glow at the mouth of the cell to look up at him. His smile didn't really reach his lips, but even so, it made her feel better.

"Korinna? You don't have to come in if you don't want to."

"Of course I do." She pulled away from him. His hand fell from where he'd cupped her cheek – she missed the warmth and certainty of that touch like an ache inside. But she swallowed against the need to throw herself into his arms and lifted her chin. "Let's go in."

The cell didn't have a door – although cell was a generous word for it. More of a long, narrow hall with high ceilings, damp and dank yet blazingly hot.

At the end of the hall was a pile of rocks where part of the ceiling had fallen to make way for the prism of red light that hung suspended from the ceiling. Inside that prism, the ancient witch's soul was trapped, forced to face the dark grey storm cloud that hung before the prism, lights flickering on its surface.

As they edged further along, keeping as far from Clodia as they could, it became clear that images played in the cloud. Images that explained why Clodia screamed and railed, her nails stretched like talons as if to tear the cloud and its images asunder if she could but reach them.

A man and a woman featured in those images. A woman with a face that reminded her of Tam's in the line of his nose and the shape of his mouth. The man had hair the colour of Tam's and a certain bearing about him that reminded her of her cupid.

His parents. Well, his father and the reincarnated soul of his mother.

Behind them, jack-o-lanterns glowed on a table laden with Halloween-inspired food, orange and black streamers; paper skeletons and fake cobwebs hung from the ceiling and every available surface. His father – Sebastio, or Bastien as he was now called – was dressed in a Highland warrior costume, while his mother, Jules, was dressed in 1950s garb, her hair styled in glossy curls. The way they looked at each other ... She swallowed hard, blinking back tears.

Suddenly, Bastien let out a whoop, hugging Jules, lifting her up to spin her around and kiss her passionately on the mouth before setting her back to place his hand over her stomach.

"She's pregnant," Tam said, voice filled with joy. "I'm going to be a brother!"

He grabbed her up and hugged her, echoing his father's movements, his joy so strong it thrummed through her despite the fact this place sucked at joy, pulling anything of light and life and happiness away from those within its walls.

Clodia screamed, a sound of fury and frustration. "No. No. You don't deserve happiness. You don't deserve to have everything when I have nothing. No. No. No!"

Clodia's torture was Jules and Bastien's happiness.

Clever Hades. She was certain he was behind this torture; it really was the kind of ingenious thing he would come up with. Many of those in the halls of the Underworld were tortured by the guilt they felt over things they did wrong in their lives – it was one of the reasons she'd run to Hades and his palace because she felt she deserved to suffer the guilt in full and where better to do that? But Tartarus was different. It couldn't punish through guilt because many of its prisoners didn't feel such a thing. Clodia certainly didn't.

So, she was tortured with what she could never have.

It seemed to be working. She was a spitting, screaming, raging mess, her soul ragged and worn; nothing close to the powerful priestess-witch she'd once been.

"Clodia." Tam moved forward, his attention now fully on the ancient priestess-witch. "Clodia," he said, voice louder this time, his power sparking, adding an irresistible tone of command.

But Clodia's attention didn't flicker for a moment from the images playing out in front of her.

Tam took another step. "Clodia, I command you to heed me." The Hells-Key glowed on his chest, power emanating from it. The guards used their Hells-Key to make the prisoners obey basic commands. Hades had obviously given Tam the ability to do the same.

Clodia's gaze flickered to him, eyes widening for a split second as if she recognised him, but then the images on the cloud changed, pulling her attention back to them, her screams of rage starting up all over again. How her voice wasn't a torn, ragged thing in her throat was beyond Korinna to understand. Maybe that was part of the torture – that her screams would be forever.

Tam frowned and looked down at the Hells-Key. "Is this thing on?" He tapped it.

She touched his hand. "It's not a microphone – and yes, it's working. But I think Clodia is so far gone, it's not touching her in the way it should."

"Then how do we get her attention?"

"Take the HeartsBlood Gem out." He raised a questioning brow. "She once believed it was hers. I don't think you'll have a problem getting her attention with it." And when he did, once he used the spell, he would have what he needed and then he would go home and be safe.

Her heart ached. Oh Gods. She thought she had more time with him. Hadn't realised how much she'd been relying on being with him for as long as she could, holding onto every moment as if it were an eternity. For her, with her days numbered, it probably was.

That time in the bubble – it wasn't enough. She'd told herself it would be, but it wasn't. Not nearly enough. But there was nothing she could do. She'd come with him to help him with this so he would give her the grimoire and the gem. She had to do as promised and let him go, even though he was the only person who ever made her feel it was okay to be herself.

"Rinna? What's wrong?"

He touched her shoulder, turning her slightly to face him. She blinked against the hot tears pressing against her eyes, mouth twisting a little. "It's almost done. Then you'll be gone."

"What are you talking about?"

She shook her head, a tear tumbling down her cheek

despite her best efforts to rope them back. She looked down at her hand captured in his and couldn't stop from twining her fingers with his, loving the strength and warmth of his grip. "Let's get what you came here for."

A cackle sounded from above them and they turned to find Clodia looking down at them, her eyes alight with evil. "So yummy. Your pain. Even with that Hells-Key doing its best to protect you from this place. From ones like me. I wonder, if I ate your soul, would it taste sweeter than that little palate cleanser you just gifted me."

"Clodia!" Tam said, fists tight by his side as he stepped closer to the prism, glaring up at her. "Leave her alone."

"How can I when she's pushing her guilt and pain out into this place? And it's enjoying it as much as I am." Her gaze moved to Korinna. "I know who you are. You are the Soteira who failed in her duty. The one who thought she knew better than the Fates and lost all those innocent souls to the Void."

Korinna gasped, her body tingling in a way it hadn't done since she'd last used her power. "You can't know that." Nobody but Hades, Demeter and Persephone knew that.

"Of course I can. Everyone down here knows what you did, Korinna Soteira."

"It wasn't her fault," Tam said, stepping in front of her. "They didn't tell her not to try to save them."

"They shouldn't have had to."

"Yes, they should! She was young and new to the role. They would have helped anybody else. And they certainly should have told her that greater magic had been wound into that line of Fate, which was what altered all her spells."

She staggered as if she'd been punched – how did Tam know all that? She'd never wanted him to know all that. But then his words caught in her mind as she turned to gape at him. "What do you mean greater magic altered my spells?"

Clodia's cackle tore through the air again. "She didn't tell you?" Her gaze pinned Korinna to the spot, stoppering the words of denial in her dry throat. "That's just delightful. Betrayed not just by him but by your Goddess as well. Honestly, you're almost too stupid to live. Perhaps that's why you're trying to die."

Korinna just gaped at her as Tam yelled, "That's a lie. Korinna wouldn't do that."

"Wouldn't she?" Clodia gestured at her, wincing a little as the red light flared around her. "Can you not feel the guilt emanating from her? The pain? The grief? So strong. So glorious. It was enough to crack through this prison and grab my attention. I wanted to gobble it all down. Feed on it. As every being down here wants to as well. Can you hear them?" She cocked her head, lips widening in a smile of madness as the screams rising from outside her cell turned to shouts of need and wanting. "They feel you. They want to gobble you up too. Your guilt and pain and grief will draw the torturers' focus away, giving the one who gets you a glorious reprieve. But they can't have you. I want you for myself. I am the one who deserves the reprieve."

"You deserve nothing," Tam spat. "Nothing but to return to your torture. After we get what we came for."

She laughed again, the sound deep, rich, enticing. "What? The truth?" Her gaze flickered to Korinna. "That they meant you to fail and didn't tell you? Not once in all these years?"

Korinna tried to deny her words, but her throat and mouth were so dry, fear and betrayal a stone in her chest she couldn't speak past. She was a fly trapped in amber – or like Clodia, trapped in the red light.

Clodia's laugh tore through the air.

"Shut up!" Tam yelled, fists shaking at his sides. "I will not let you torment her with your half-truths."

Clodia's mouth widened in an horrific smile, eyes dancing with unholy light. "Oh, this is too wonderful. That the son of my greatest enemies can be so clueless about the one he loves. It's delicious."

"I said shut up," he snarled at the same time Korinna choked out, "You really do love me?"

His focus snapped to Korinna, indigo eyes glowing in the red-dark of the cavern. "Of course I do. I've always loved you. Since the first day I saw you at the camp."

"But ... you're a cupid."

"You believed that old wives' tale? All cupids are capable of loving – even me. I just can never receive it because of my curse. But I do love you even though I know you can never love me."

She shook her head slowly, all other worries swept away under the tsunami of his admission. "But ... that's not right. I do. Love you. I've always loved you too."

He grabbed her shoulders, his blue-blue gaze searching deep within hers. "You love me? How is that possible? It can't be true."

"It is. But you shouldn't love me. I don't ... I don't deserve it."

"What are you talking about? If anyone doesn't deserve your love, it's me."

Clodia's cackle cracked between them, tearing their gazes from each other and back to her. "How sweet. Two deluded souls so caught up in your own misgivings that you missed the fact you are both wrong. You were used as a patsy," she said, pointing at Korinna. "And your curse isn't what you think it is," she said, gaze flickering over him. "I

128

would think you'd learned that after what happened to your parents, cupid. But please, keep up this little drama. Your pain is filling me up all the way over here. Yummy."

Korinna glared at her. "We're not here for your edification."

"Really? Because it's the only way you get to have what you want — all this drama of emotion is bringing me a clarity I've not felt for the Hells-centuries I've been trapped here. And isn't that what you need? Me in my right mind so I can help you?"

Tam growled. "What do you mean I'm wrong about the curse? What does it have to do with my parents?"

Clodia wagged her finger. "That's not what you're here for, is it?"

"You don't know what we're here for."

"Don't I?"

"Then tell us. Share with us what you know of the curse and where you hid my mother's powers."

"What about the lost souls *she's* aiming to find?" she asked, bony finger jabbing towards Korinna.

"What are you talking about?" He glanced at Korinna.

She shrugged, hoping he believed she was as clueless about Clodia's meaning as he was.

"So many misunderstandings between you. So many secrets and lies needing to be exposed."

"No!" Korinna lurched forward. "It is you who are full of secrets and lies."

"It takes a liar to know a liar." Her eyes gleamed darkly red as she swept her gaze over Korinna.

She trembled, hands clenching at her sides, unable to do anything to stop the ancient priestess-witch.

Clodia laughed. "Use your power, little witch. Unleash it as you did all those years ago. There's no magical energy of the greater Gods waiting to subvert it here. It's the only way to stop me."

"No," Korinna gasped. The witch couldn't be right. It *had* been her. Persephone would have told her if some greater magic had been at play.

"Ahh, but what of your lost souls? How will you get them to Elysium if not with a final burst of magic?"

Korinna shook her head, aware that Tam was looking at her with confusion. "I will use it then. Only then."

"Why then and not now?"

She tried to shut her mouth, but it was like the truth was being pulled out of her. This place. It had to be this place. So it could excel in its torture. "Because after that, nothing will matter. The souls will be safe."

"And you?"

She tried to fight it, but the words forced their way up, squeezed out her mouth on a hated breath. "I will be gone."

CHAPTER
THIRTEEN

Tamuel stared at Rinna, her words a violent storm in his mind, his heart. "No. You can't."

"I have to," she said, bitterly, her tone a raw aching thing. "There's no other way."

"But ... I saw your memories when we hid from the wraiths. Felt your guilt and pain. I understand how terrible it's been for you, Rinna, but how can you think to ...?" He shook his head, unable to say the words.

Tears spilled from her eyes, her face a study in agony. "I wouldn't have. Not if I'd known you'd come back to me. That you did love me."

"Then take it back."

"I can't, any more than I can take back the spell that doomed those souls."

"Don't you mean the spell an Old One screwed with so that it wouldn't work?"

"No. That's not right." She jabbed a finger at Clodia. "You're lying."

"No, I'm not," Clodia snapped. "He's not the only one who's cursed."

"What do you mean?"

Her smile slowly widened. "They were always jealous of those of us with more potential than they have. It's why I landed here. Why they did what they did to you. It's quite clever if you think about it. You take yourself out of the picture and they keep their hands clean. You were just too stupid and self-involved to see it." She pouted. "And just when you've discovered your true love. Too bad, so sad."

"No," Tamuel said, grabbing Rinna close against him. She was stiff, unyielding. Panic tightened his chest, breath catching in his throat. "No. There has to be another way."

"You can't stop it," Rinna said, her words a rumble against his chest. "I made a vow to make right what I did wrong."

"But it wasn't your fault. An Old One screwed with your spells. You have to see that. Hells, even *she* sees that." He jabbed a finger towards Clodia, who cackled again.

She closed her eyes. "Even if that's true, it doesn't change the fact those souls have to be saved and I vowed to save them. The spell requires a lifeforce in exchange." Her lip trembled, tears streaking down her face as she opened her eyes to look up at him. "I love you more than life itself; would do anything to be with you, but—" She choked on the words, struggling for a moment before she said softly, "I made a vow. I wish I hadn't now, but I did. There's no escaping it." Her topaz eyes should have reflected the red light of Clodia's prison, but they didn't. They glowed with the eternal golden light of her power and something else.

Her love. For him.

It *was* true. How it was possible with his curse, he wasn't certain, but he couldn't deny the reality of it. The glow of it washed over him, connecting with him, pulling him into the depths of her, until he wasn't sure where he ended and she began. Her love was everything. It was truth and power and everything good.

She couldn't die. "No," he said again. "I won't let you. You need to come with me. We'll find another way. We'll visit all the Realms."

"I can't. I'm tethered here. I couldn't trust in my power when I made my vow, so I used the power of the Death Realms as a proxy. When the Eternal Well accepted my vow, it bound me to this place until I meet my destiny. I belong down here. You don'—"

He put his finger over her mouth. "I will not let you be stuck down here any longer. I will not let you die to fulfil your agreement with the Eternal Well when it was never your fault in the first place. You don't owe those souls your life. We'll find an answer. There's bound to be something in the Eleusinian Mysteries aside from the destructive spell you want to use. And this. We have this." He pulled the HeartsBlood Gem from his shirt.

"Oh, my pretty, powerful friend," Clodia screeched. "You brought her to me."

"I didn't bring the HeartsBlood Gem for you. I brought it to use against you."

Clodia's eyes glowed. "It won't respond to you, stupid cupid. It's filled with Goddess-given power. It will only connect with feminine energy. So, *she* will have to use it."

"Rinna says I'll be able to use it as long as she's touching it."

"Does she now. Well, she'd be W-R-O-N-G, wrong. She would need to use her own power, and a significant amount of it to boot to override my will."

"But I can't," Rinna said, a sob in her voice. "I need to hoard as much of my power as I can for my final spell."

Clodia wagged her finger. "True. Pity you kept your

powers subdued all these years, rusty and nowhere what they should be. Especially given you used such a large portion of them keeping *him* safe; fulfilling *his* quest."

Rinna's eyes widened. "That's not true."

"Isn't it? You've been leaking power ever since you saw him. You leaked it in the tunnels to help shield him from the wraiths; to speed you on your journey. It poured from you when you fucked him, and again when you helped him to stop you both from falling into the abyss. And it was your power that found the tunnel that led straight to the Gates of Tartarus. We all felt it down here through your entire journey. It was glorious. And a pathetic waste of talent."

"That's a lie! Tam did that all himself and ... I ... I'd know if I used my power."

"If you don't believe me, just feel inside. Your reserves of power are not enough to power the spell you wish to use. Not any time soon. You've wasted it on him." She pouted. "Who knows what will happen to those poor souls if they're in the Void much longer. When I saw them after his mother trapped me in there, they were getting rather ragged."

Rinna gasped. "You saw them?"

A manic smile replaced the pout. "Of course. And I can take you to them ... but only if you do what I need you to do first."

"I thought you said I didn't have enough power."

"You have enough to do what I need you to do. And if you do my bidding, then I'll help you save those souls."

"You only help yourself." Tamuel grabbed Rinna's hands, trying to turn her away from staring at the witch-bitch, the expression of devastation on her face a different kind of torture. "We will find a way," he said. "There is always a loophole. You won't need to use all your powers and you won't have to die. I won't allow it."

"Allow it? Listen to you. Being all man-like and trying to play the hero," Clodia said. "But you can fix nothing. Only I know the way for her to succeed in her vow without giving everything. And maybe, just maybe, you might even be able to be with him. Although, why you'd want to is beyo—"

"What is your price?"

"Rinna, you can't listen to her."

Clodia smiled slowly, her gaze never leaving Rinna. "Surely my freedom is a small payment for the chance to live and be with cupid-boy forever?"

"Rinna, we can't set her free."

"*You* can't. But *she* can."

Rinna shook her head, gaze pinned on Clodia. "Even if what you say is true and my power is now not enough, I've looked and looked. There is no other way. My soul has to power the spell to open the rift and find the souls because I canted the spell that sent them there."

"True. But, you haven't been where I've been. You haven't seen what I've seen. You have no idea what can be done, especially with a little bit of Goddess-given power. Only I do. And I vow, if you free me, I will go to the Void and release those souls and send them to Elysium for you."

"Why would you want to go back to the Void."

She smiled. "That's for me to know and you to … wonder about for now."

He gripped Rinna's shoulders, turned her towards him. "Don't listen to her. She's a liar. We can use the Hearts-Blood Gem, get her to tell us what we need—"

The alarm shriek of the chronometer cut him off.

"*The veil has thinned. Alignment finalised. The Under-world's position has changed. Time has shifted. The clocks will strike twelve on All Hallows' Eve in two minutes Earthly Realm time. Fifteen minutes Tartarus time. You have fifteen minutes to return. Countdown has begun."*

Korinna's gaze snapped to him, grabbing at his arm, fingers fumbling to undo the band of the chronometer. "You've run out of time. Give me the HeartsBlood Gem. I'll find some way of getting her to tell me what you came here for and get the information to you. But you have to go. Carve the spell. Do it now."

He grabbed her hands, stopped her from trying to remove the chronometer so he could carve the spell on his wrist. "I'm not leaving without you, my love."

She gripped his hands, leaned up and pressed her lips against his. "I can't let you do that. I can't let you make that sacrifice for me."

"That's not your choice to make."

"Yes, it is. I thought for so long I couldn't trust my choices. But I can. You helped show me that. You've saved me in ways you can't know. Now let me save you."

She kissed him again before he could protest, then before he could pull her close, she was gone.

He stumbled as the force of the magic she'd used to transport herself across the cavern pushed him back a step. "Rinna, no!" He raced after her, but she leaped to the top of the pile of rocks before he'd made it a couple of steps.

He flung his magic towards her, intending to stop her, but it bounced off the golden glow of power now emanating from her like a shield – how had he not realised that was her golden glow working alongside his magic earlier? Her power that had made his so much stronger? Her power helping to make him feel whole?

She flung herself from the top rock towards the prism,

slamming one hand towards it, while the other pointed at him.

"Rinna, no!"

Light exploded around them, blinding him as power smacked him in the chest. He slammed into the jagged rock wall behind him; sharp rocks tore through tunic and skin. He ignored the pain – he'd known worse – and tried to push off the wall. But the wave of power wouldn't let him. Against his chest, the HeartsBlood Gem glowed brightly, pulsing with the power that flowed through it, keeping him pinned. He used his cupid and warlock power to fight its hold, but for every inch he fought to move forward, another pulse struck, forcing him back.

She was strong, so strong. Clodia was right about one thing – Rinna was strong enough to break the priestess-witch free, something only a very powerful God should be able to do. Her magic had changed, become something other than what it had been – maybe because she'd been living down here for too long; maybe because of what she'd done; maybe because it was always going to get stronger and change – and maybe that's why some Old One had screwed with her power and brought her to this point of thinking she deserved death.

Even so, she would have to drain herself dry to free Clodia from her prison. And that alone could kill her.

"Rinna! Stop!" The light had become so bright he couldn't see her, but he could hear her scream of pain and anguish, torn from her as she forced her magic to break the prism. "Rinna, stop. Please, stop."

There was an ear-piercing wail, an almighty crack. Then the noise and light disappeared.

He fell away from the wall, slamming onto his knees, light-blinded, ears ringing. Trying to blink away the light-shadow, he shook his head to clear the ringing from his ears. "Rinna?" She didn't answer. The only sound was cackling.

Clodia!

He rubbed his eyes, vision returning enough to see that Clodia was out of the prism, looking at the body lying on the ground at her feet. The ancient witch looked up at him as she brushed at her tattered tunic, frowning. "Well, that's a problem."

CHAPTER
FOURTEEN

He didn't take any notice of Clodia, his attention solely on his love. Every part of him screamed in pain as he pushed to his feet then stumbled one step after another towards Rinna, his gaze never leaving her.

Smoke rose in wisps off the material of her tunic. Blood ran from a gash on her forehead. One leg and arm lay at a strange angle.

Still. So still. He couldn't even tell if she was breathing.

"Rinna," he said, her name a sob in his throat as he tripped over his feet, agony tearing through his damaged back from shoulder to hip with each step. But he didn't care, his entire attention on Rinna as he came down on his knees in the rough dirt beside her. "Why did you do that, my love?"

She didn't stir, but her chest rose up then down, the motion ragged. She was still alive. He reached for her, but hesitated, not wanting to cause her more injury. Instead, he leaned down, kissed her gently, hoping she would waken at his touch.

"You know you two are as sickening as your parents."

He glared up at the witch who'd caused this. "What did you do?"

She placed a hand on her chest. "Moi? I did nothing. She was the one who did it all. She freed me."

"Then why are you still here?"

Her eyes glittered. "There is something more I need."

"Ten minutes until the veil closes and you are trapped," the chronometer chimed in warning.

He ignored it. "I don't care about what you need. Now go and do as you vowed and let me save her."

Clodia's smile widened. "Ah, just a little problem with that." She pointed at Rinna. "Her power opened my prison, but she poured too much of it into shielding you. That backlash should have killed you. Now, to get out of here and make myself a body, I need power. Your cupid power will suffice. You opened the portal to get here with it, and along with the spell you got from that nifty grimoire those Eleusinian nuts wrote, it's all I need to get back."

"I will never give it to you. I will never set you free."

She crouched down in front of him. "Not even if it means letting her free of her vow?" She reached out as if to touch Rinna, but he slapped her hand away. She smiled, slow, nasty. "Not even if it means being able to take her with you so you can save her?"

"I can't take her with me. She's tethered here."

"The only thing tethering her here is that vow. But who's to say the Eternal Well would be just as happy for someone else to do it? She saw the truth in that," she said, pointing at Rinna. "Would you let her sacrifice be for nothing? I'm far more capable of completing her vow than anyone else. Give me what I want and that vow disappears. You can take her; save her. Give me what I need to gain my

freedom and I will take up the burden of her vow. Agreed?"
She stuck out her hand.

He stared at her. She was a liar, but something in her face told him she wasn't lying about this. He knew he shouldn't do this; knew she should never be allowed to go free after what she'd done; knew if she got free, she wouldn't cease her grasp for power. But ...

He looked down at Rinna. Her breathing laboured more with every minute he allowed to pass. He might be able to use the Hells-Key to call on Hades to help, but ... he was in the Earthly Realm at Persephone's party and he had no idea how to jerry-rig the spells on the Hells-Key to reach him there.

He took Clodia's hand. "Agreed."

Power burned along his arm, twining up hers, binding them to the promise.

When the binding was done, she pulled her hand from his. "Excellent. Now, to the good stuff." She clapped her hands. Her eyes glowed black.

Something tore deep inside him. He gasped, bending double at the pain that overrode the cuts and gashes on his back.

"Hurts, doesn't it? It's the very least you deserve for being part of taking what was mine. Now the spell." He cried out as something blunt jabbed into his mind, pushing, digging. "Ah, there it is." She began to carve the sigil on her wrist with a jagged stone she picked up from the floor. "Those Eleusinian priestesses were clever to bond blood magic with life magic. It should be unstable but it's not. Ah, one little change – I don't want to end up where you departed from, do I? There, that should do. Now, give me the rest." She reached out her hands, making a gathering motion. Something tore inside him, the pain so great, he could barely breathe.

"Ugh. So much love and hope and sacrifice in your soul, it sickens me."

"I hope you choke on it," he managed to gasp.

She only smiled at him, moving her hands faster, the threads of his amethyst cupid power glowing almost blackly-purple in the red light of the broken prism, shards of which still hung above them and lay on the floor, shattered, around them.

The pain intensified, blackness edging his vision. "I will find you. And I will get back what is mine."

"Now, now, don't be like that. I'm doing you a favour. When you are no longer a cupid, you will no longer be tied to your curse."

"You're lying. The curse is gone. She loves me. I don't know how but ..." He blinked. Clodia had said he didn't understand his curse. That he'd not learned from his parents. That could only mean one thing ... "She's my soulmate." The loophole Eros had woven into his curse. She was the cracked piece of mirror – the imperfect cursed soul equal and opposite to his. Together, they were whole. No longer soul cursed. They were free. That was why she'd always loved him. And he'd been too stupid to realise. Well, he'd make up to her for that when he got her out of here and saved her.

"How can you still hope when all hope is gone?" Clodia smiled, her motions jerky, vicious, as she manipulated his power, pulling it into her in larger chunks.

He gasped, the pain almost making him black out. But he held on; for Rinna if not for himself.

The chronometer screeched its five-minute warning.

"Time to go," Clodia said, yanking the final dregs of

cupid power from him. He collapsed over Rinna as the evil witch waved her hand. Light flared brightly overhead and the remaining shards of the prism exploded. Somehow, despite the pain slicing through him, he used his warlock power and flung a shield around them to protect Rinna from the dangerously sharp slithers of light. Clodia might have taken his cupid power, a power fuelled by one of the strongest magics known to Gods or man – love – but she hadn't taken the warlock power he had from his mother.

The bitch-witch probably thought it was weak because it was untrained. But it wasn't. Especially when he was with Rinna.

He held the shield tight over them as the prism rained around them.

The chronometer buzzed again – four minutes.

Then the light vanished, replaced by the dark-red glow of the caverns.

He looked up. Clodia was gone.

A roar sounded deep in the earth, making the cavern tremble and shake. Was it an alarm sounding to indicate an escaped prisoner? Or was it Tartarus' anger over her escape? Did it even matter? He'd almost run out of time. He had to get them out of here. Clodia might have thought by taking his cupid powers she'd got what she needed to escape, thereby trapping them both here, but she hadn't.

He hadn't realised it until now, but it had been his warlock powers that allowed him to tap into the ark under the Stevens' library and get him here – like called to like after all. And it was his warlock power – still connected to that well of magic – that would get him and Rinna back home where he could call for help to save her.

Rubble fell from the roof of the cavern. The shield sparked with every hit; amethyst and gold. He tightened his control, amazed doing so barely took anything from him at all. Just as well – he needed everything to get them home.

The roar became louder, rumbling around them, making everything shake and shake until it looked like the walls and roof and floor were moving liquid. The sound of that roar – pure rage.

He empathised with that rage. Felt something like it inside him. He would use it to track down Clodia, to capture her with the HeartsBlood Gem and make her tell him everything he needed to know to help him finish his quest. She might have thought to have outwitted him, but she hadn't. He had only agreed to give her what she needed to get out of this cell; he hadn't agreed to anything else.

But first, he had to get them back; he had to save Rinna. Thank the Gods he no longer had to go into his memory to remember the spell or change it as needed to travel from this place: in taking it from his mind, Clodia had unwittingly shown him exactly what he needed to do.

The chronometer buzzed the two-minute countdown.

Hurriedly, he removed the chronometer, shoving it into his pocket, then cut open his wrist with the knife Rinna had put in his backpack and drew the sigil on his wrist along with the change in destination, aware with every line he was running out of time.

One minute.

He began carving the sigil into Rinna's wrist.

Thirty seconds.

He picked her limp body up, holding her close, then as the chronometer counted down from ten, he canted the spell from the Eleusinian Mysteries.

Power gathered in him, punching through his skin, out of the sigils, the pain almost blinding. The world shifted, portals opening up around him, showing him all the

Realms that could be reached through the veil if one only had the will and the right spell to traverse them.

Sensing more than seeing the one he needed, he stepped forward, grunting as Tartarus tried to pull him back, tried to keep him in its embrace. Or was it trying to keep Rinna? It couldn't have her.

He tightened his grip around his love as the chronometer intoned, "2, 1 ..." and threw himself forward, using up the last reserves of power he had in him, hoping he wasn't too late.

CHAPTER
FIFTEEN

Darkness surrounded Korinna. She was falling, falling. And as she fell, the darkness squeezed in around her. Smashing into Clodia's prison had been painful, a sensation like being torn asunder, but this ... this was something else. Like she was still in her body, being pulled out of it a bit at a time.

Oh Gods. It hurt. It hurt. She wanted to scream, but had no voice.

The squeezing intensified, then suddenly, it was gone.

Cool dark surrounded her.

Was it supposed to feel like this – her soul torn from her body and sent down into the Underworld? She'd not expected it to feel like sunshine and roses, but she'd not expected this.

A voice shouted in the dark, alongside a sensation of being picked up and carried then placed somewhere softer. Kinder.

It sounded like Tam.

Tam.

Her heart ached at the thought that she would never

see him again. Never be with him again. His soul was bound for Elysium far in the future when it was finally his time to pass through the veil of death, whereas hers—

Her soul cried out at the unfairness. She'd thought she deserved this, but the loss of those souls – she knew now it wasn't her fault. She shouldn't be made to pay. She deserved love. As did he.

He loved her. She loved him. She wanted a life with him more than she'd ever wanted anything. But it didn't matter. She'd sacrificed to save him and now she was dead.

The darkness disappeared as light flickered and shifted behind her lids.

"Help. Help. She's barely breathing." Tam's voice rose out of the watery depths of noise, becoming clearer.

No. He couldn't be here. She'd saved him – hadn't she?

Yes. Yes, she had. So … this was her punishment. To show her what she could have had – if only she'd not been so stupid as to see what he had seen so clearly when he'd somehow seen her memories – then yank it from her.

"Here, let me in." Another voice. Deeper than Tam's and yet achingly similar.

Something warm touched her chest, radiating outward. She would have cried out at the shock of it, but didn't seem to be able to move or speak.

"Foolish boy." An older voice. A woman. "What were you thinking? To use such a spell on such a night."

"Don't lecture him, Grandmama." A younger woman's voice, patient, gentle. "I think he's been through enough. How is she, Bas? Is she breathing?"

The warmth wrapped around Korinna, pushing into her skin, into her muscles and veins and nerves, probing. "She's alive," the deeper male voice said – Bas? "But her injuries are severe. What the hell happened, son?"

"She gave her powers to allow Clodia to escape," Tam answered.

"Why would she do that!?"

"Violetta! Calm down. Let him tell us why he brought her here."

"She did it to complete a vow," Tam continued. "And I think, to save me. To give me the reason to remember the spell and get back here."

"Clodia is free?" the younger woman asked, her voice an aching whisper.

"Yes. I couldn't stop her."

"It will be all right, Julianna," the older woman – Violetta – said.

Julianna? Bas? Violetta? This was Tam's family. But why would her punishment show her this? Was she not in Hell being tortured? If not, then where in the Realms was she?

"Violetta is right, Jules. We won't let her get anywhere near you. Besides, Clodia is a spirit and she still has to find a way out of the Underworld."

"She's not a spirit anymore. She took my powers and used them to enact the spell from the Eleusinian Mysteries Grimoire and become corporeal."

"The Eleusinian Mysteries Grimoire! How did you get your hands on that, boy?"

"That doesn't matter, Violetta. What matters is that she's corporeal. Hades will be furious."

"Who cares about that overbearing bore? You and your father can deal with him, Bas. But a grimoire of that much power in the wrong hands—"

"My son is hardly the wrong hands, Violetta!"

"She took your powers?" Jules said softly, and even though it was barely a whisper, it cut across Bas and Violetta's arguing. "Oh, Tamuel."

"Only my cupid ones."

"Oh, son."

"Don't feel sorry for me. I gave of them freely in a bargain to save Rinna," Tam said grimly. "Dad? How is she? Can you heal her?"

"I can try, but it's going to take some time. Why don't you lie down and get some rest yourself? You look like you're about to fall down."

"He looks like skin and bone," Jules said, her voice a throb of caring. "You're lucky she didn't kill you when she took your powers."

"I had no choice. I had to save Rinna."

"You're just like your mother," Violetta said gruffly.

"No, I'm not. I still have my warlock powers. That's what got me back. What helped get Rinna here. You have to save her, Dad."

"She's very important to you then?" Jules asked softly, her voice accompanying a sweep of movement over Korinna's brow, through her hair; a soothing, caring touch.

Silence, then, "She's my best friend and the love of my life. My soulmate. She broke my curse. I would die for her."

She'd broken his curse?

"Oh, son." The soft sounds that indicated someone was being hugged, tears were being shed. "I'm so happy that the horrible curse Eros put on you has been broken. So happy you have found your soulmate."

Soulmate? They were soulmates? She wanted to look in his eyes, see the truth there, but the warmth had moved, shifting to concentrate on her leg, her arm, her chest; pain she hadn't noticed until now began to fire through her. She wanted to scream as bones snapped and reshaped inside her, but still couldn't open her eyes let alone make a sound or move.

A hand grasped hers – Tam's – and a calming tingle shot through her veins, alleviating the agony until it was a low throb of pain. She would have sobbed with relief but still nothing came. Something warm and hard was placed on her chest. "Rinna. Please come back to me. I love you. We have our future to plan together."

Then darkness took over her.

CHAPTER
SIXTEEN

Korinna woke to a bright light glowing red behind her closed lids. Warmth aligned along her back and legs and across her chest. A lovely warmth she wanted to curl into and never let go.

That warmth moved, shifting against her. A puff of breath against her neck.

She opened heavy lids and looked down. A male arm, its strong lines and fine dusting of dark hair, curled around her waist. Her fingers wrapped around that arm, hugging it to her. A fine scar ran over the back of his wrist and down onto a large, masculine hand with long, fine fingers currently cupping her breast.

She'd know that hand and arm anywhere.

Tam.

He was here? No. No. He couldn't be here. She'd saved him. She'd saved him.

"Shh, shh." His arm tightened around her as she jerked, panic taking her breath. "It's just a nightmare." A kiss to her neck then to her head, her ear, her forehead as he shifted behind her, moving to roll her onto her back.

He hung over her, his auburn hair bed-tousled, a hesitant smile on his lips as their gazes met.

"You were supposed to live." Her lip trembled.

"Hey, hey," he said, kissing the tremble away, his hand running up and down her side, chasing zaps of lightning along her skin. "I did. We both did. Although it was a close thing for you." He kissed her again and when he pulled away, his indigo eyes were dark with remembered grief. "Don't ever do that to me again." His other hand caressed her cheek, her brow, stroking her hair away from her face. She wanted to melt under his touch.

But ... "How is it possible?" She reached up, touched his face, her thumbs sweeping over his cheek, touching the grey hollow under his eyes before moving down to shape over his lips. He pressed a kiss against the tips, making them tingle. "You're alive. You're safe."

"And so are you. And free. We found the loophole. Your vow is now Clodia's to complete. And the moment she took it, your tether to the Underworld broke. I brought you to my family home to heal."

"But you didn't get your answer ... and that's all my fault."

"Not your fault. And now you are here to help me on my quest. Together we can track Clodia down and get my mother's powers back. Just like together we broke my curse."

"Oh." She remembered the conversation she'd heard after she thought she'd died when the pain was so bad. But she hadn't died. She'd been clinging onto life – clinging onto Tam, as he'd clung onto her, holding her with him. "We're soulmates." Her mouth twisted.

"That's supposed to make you happy."

"It does. So happy."

"So these are happy tears?" He swept his thumb across her face.

"Yes. What about these?" she asked, brushing her fingers across his cheek, capturing a tear that had fallen from his glorious eyes.

"The happiest of tears."

She reached up and pulled him down to her, losing herself in his kiss, in the feel of his hands as they roved over her, the feel of him under her fingers, delighted to find he had slept without a top on. She wished he didn't have his pants on.

"Hey!" he sat bolt upright, now completely naked. "You've got magic? How?"

He stared down at her, confusion all over his handsome face.

She didn't blame him. She was just as confused. She sat up slowly, leaning against the pillows stacked against the head of the huge comfortable bed they were in – his bed. "I've got magic." She'd thrown it all at Clodia's prison, to break it, except what she'd channelled to protect Tam. Her eyes flared wide as they went to his chest – bare of the Hells-Key and the HeartsBlood Gem. "The gem. Where's the gem?"

"Here." He touched between her breasts. "You're wearing it."

She looked down. It glowed softly red against the sheets she'd pulled up around her when she sat up. She hadn't even realised it was there.

"What has the gem to do with it?"

She took it in her hand. It pulsed at her touch, a voice sounding in her head, *"Hello friend. I saved it for you."*

"Oh."

"What?"

She held it out to him. "Touch it." He raised a brow but did as she bid. The gem glowed for him too, but when she dropped her hand, leaving it only clasped in his, the glow faded. She put her hand on it again. It pulsed brightly, almost happily. "Oh. I understand."

"What? I don't understand."

She met Tam's gaze. "It caught the magic I sent to you. I thought it would act as a conduit, sending the magic into you, so it was yours. So you could use it without me." An image flashed before her: of him calling for her, trying to get to her, his entire attention on her, desperate to stop her from sacrificing herself. "I didn't even know it would work – I had no time to prepare the stone properly. But it did it. It took my power and gave it to you." She frowned slightly. "But then, somehow, it gave it back to me. I don't understand how?"

He stared down at the gem, a small smile curling the corner of his mouth. "Clever, sneaky thing."

"What? Why?"

He met her gaze. "When my dad was healing you, I heard a voice telling me I had to put the gem on you and hold on. I didn't even question it. I just did it. It must have transferred the power then, when my attention was solely on you."

"But you didn't incant the spell."

"I didn't need to." His smile widened. "It responded to the strongest spell of all."

"Love," she whispered.

"Love," he repeated.

They held the HeartsBlood Gem in their hands, the red glow brightening as a whisper, so faint to be almost unheard, sounded around them. *Soul cursed you both may have been, but love blessed is what you are now. With that love, you will do great things."*

"Is that the gem?" Tam asked.

"I think it is." They stared at it, wonderingly, their fingers tightening simultaneously. "Speak to us again."

The gem glowed brighter, faded, then glowed again, the voice louder this time, musically lyrical and yet husky and deep. *"You must find Clodia. You must bring her to justice. You must save us all from what she will do with a cupid's magic and the Goddess-given powers stolen from Julianna Stevens that she will go after now she's free."*

"But how?" Korinna asked, her voice croaking in surprise.

"I will guide you." The voice became faint again. *"But first, you must set me free."*

They stared at the gem, then each other, then back to the gem. "How do we do that?"

The gem's glow fluttered. The voice came, but was so soft, so distant, Korinna couldn't hear what it said. "I can't hear you." She looked up at Tam; he shrugged. "Say it again. Tell us how we can free you? How can you help us to find Clodia and do what we have to do?"

"Build your power," the voice whispered, only just loud enough that she caught the words.

She shook her head slowly, whispering, "I can't." Her powers had always been so big, and now, they were a quarter of that; enough to do simple spells but no more. Despite what Tam and Clodia had told her, she didn't know if she could trust herself to make the right decisions if her powers were returned to her in full. Look at the mess she'd made about the vow for one!

The gem fluttered brighter, the voice sounding louder. *"You can. Your power is not the source of your grief, it is its salvation. Trust in yourself. Trust in your love. Both of you. It will help more than you know. Strengthen yourself and all will be revealed. Even perhaps the source of what has tormented your souls and caused you to be separated this long."*

"How? When?"

The gem glowed sluggishly in their hands. Korinna gripped Tam's other hand, their gazes meeting, worried. Then a whisper sounded around them, distant and echoing. *"Share your love. Build the powers you were both left using family, hearth and home as your centre, as your strength. When the world renews and the hare and the Goddess of rebirth are in the zenith, my power will be at its height. In the days of Oestra, I will come back and tell you what must be done."*

"That long? But Clodia?"

"She can do nothing until then. Your mate was clever. He did not let on that the power she stole from him was not what powered the portal spell. She escaped, but only to the last place she had been. She is trapped once more in the Void without the power to get out. Even if she finds Julianna's Goddess-given powers, she will be unable to do anything until the days of Oestra when all power renews. Until then, protect each other and those you love. And keep me safe."

Tam looked deeply into Korinna's eyes and then back down at the gem. "I have the perfect place."

Lifting the gem, her fingers still entwined with his, he put the gem against his chest and canted:

> *"With powerful magic, the greatest of all*
> *Keep this gem safe from evil and thrall*
> *Wrapped in the embrace of my healed heart*
> *Protected by the love of souls no longer apart*
> *A part of her, a part of me*
> *Three become one, until one becomes three.*

Bound by the waning power of All Hallows' Eve
Willed with our love, so mote it be."

The gem glowed red and gold as the spell wound around their hands.

She gaped at him. "How?" He'd just used a spell she'd only ever heard rumour of.

"Demeter gave it to me long ago, the day Eros came to take me back. She said she thought I might one day need it."

"But it will only work between those whose love is true and deserved."

"Exactly."

The gem pulsed hot in their hands, and slowly melded with his flesh, close to where the Hells-Key had been not so long ago.

She hadn't admitted it, but there had been a kernel of doubt. Now ...

She sucked in a breath and met his gaze. They had a lot to discuss; a lot to unwind of their pasts and who had tried to keep them apart; of who had used her to take the blame and why; and why nobody had told her that until Tam and Clodia had. There was also a lot to figure out about what the HeartsBlood Gem had told them. But none of that mattered right now. All that mattered was what he was doing. What it meant.

She leaned forward and pressed her lips against his. "I love you," she breathed as she pulled back.

"As I love you."

He kissed her again, and she lost herself in the flavour of him, of the sensation pulsing through her as his tongue brushed over hers. Slowly, she became aware the heat had gone, her fingers flush against the smooth skin of his chest.

She pulled back a little and looked down.

The gem had vanished inside his chest, a faint pulsing glow the only sign it was there.

She looked up at him and smiled. "It's where it's meant to be." The HeartsBlood Gem, held safe with their love.

"For now."

"For now."

"Do you really believe we can do it?"

He nodded. "I believe we can do anything, together. And with the HeartsBlood Gem's help, we'll get all of the stolen power back, we'll make certain Clodia sent your lost souls to Elysium, we'll free the spirit from the gem and then we will have our HEA."

"HEA?"

He rolled his eyes. "How can someone so well-read not know HEA is Happy Ever After."

"I never read fairy tales. I never believed my prince would come to save me."

"He didn't. Well, not until after the princess first saved him."

"Yes, I did, didn't I?" She put her other hand against the warm strength of his chest, looking deeply into his eyes. "Our Happy Ever After. I like the sound of that."

"So do I."

They kissed again for long moments, until she pulled back. "What are we going to tell Hades? And Persephone?"

He groaned dramatically and fell back into the pillows behind her. "Did you have to bring that up now?"

She patted him on his chest. "Don't worry. I'll save you from their wrath."

"You better. No point me ending up dead now."

"I won't let him touch a hair on your precious head."

158

"So fierce." He tackled her to the bed, kissed her laughter from her lips. "I love you."

"I love you."

He looked down at his chest then back at her, his smile widening. "No longer soul cursed, but love blessed."

"Forever."

"Amen to that."

∼

THANK you for reading the first part of Tamuel and Korinna's story. I hope you enjoyed it. There's still lots more excitement and discovery, passion and sexy-times, action and evil to fight for this cupid and his soulmate.

To find out what happens next, read on for the first Chapter of *Blood Cursed:*

BLOOD CURSED

LEISL LEIGHTON

THE CURSE OF ILIA

Stolen and tricked and bound to the heart,
Yet blessed to use the power of home and hearth
Waiting and scheming for a way to depart
That which bound me by love's false start.
Only those like me, cursed yet kind,
Can help to break the bonds that bind,
Truth-seekers powered to free spirit and mind,
And question the false-certainty of Gods that blind:
That love is not that which will cause the fall,
But the thing that should succour and save us all.
This is my curse uttered unto thee,
Trapped, used and Gods-cursed, through eternity.
I await the soul and blood cursed to set me free
So I utter it to the universe, so mote it be.
Hidden incantation in the lost Eleusinian Mysteries
Grimoire

CHAPTER
ONE

Korinna Soteira kissed her soulmate, Tamuel, goodbye. "Good luck and take care," she said, lips lingering on his.

"Are you sure you don't want to come?"

Gods, she did. She hated being apart from him. Just as he hated being apart from her. Every time he had to track down a lead, he begged her to come with him, but ...

She glanced at the chronometer she'd placed on the wall next to Jules' train station clock. Only a month until the first day of Oestra. Twenty-eight days left to discover what they'd failed to discover in the last five months. She frowned. "It doesn't make sense for both of us to go off tracking down leads. Just as it doesn't make sense for both of us to stay and do research."

"Yeah, yeah. Divide and conquer – right? But it sucks."

She kissed his pouting lips. "I know." But they didn't have the time not to divide and conquer. They had to find a way to channel their powers together without endangering themselves and everyone else – especially when they added the energy of Oestra into the mix. If they didn't, they wouldn't be able to release the spirit from the HeartsBlood Gem. And without her, they'd never defeat the evil Priestess-witch Clodia when she came out of the Void the first night of Oestra. But so far, nada. "Are you sure the gem's spirit hasn't told you anything?"

He touched the place in his chest where he'd magically spelled the gem to live so as to keep it safe after the events of Halloween. "Not anything we can use in regard to this."

"But she is talking to you? Has she told you more about how powerful Clodia is likely to be? She was strong when your mother fought her, and it took Jules sacrificing her power to defeat her and push her into the Void. But now ... I mean, does she still have some of my power? Yours? Will she be able to use the power your mother sacrificed when she pushed her into the Void? Will she be able to draw on the power of Oestra as we will be doing?" She could feel the questions rushing out of her, but couldn't help it. There was just too much they still didn't know.

"I don't know." His hands smoothed down her arms in a calming motion.

"Ask her."

"I have," he said, raking his hand through his hair, ruffling his curls. "The only thing she says is that with our powers combined, plus what we can gather from Ostara rising, we should be able to defeat her."

"Should? Can't she give us more certainty than that?"

"Apparently not."

She bit her lip. "I thought when we started this, she'd be there to help us, to steer us in the right direction. But all she gave us was romanticised waffle that hasn't helped at all. *'Your power is not the source of your grief, it is its salvation.'* What the Hells does that really mean? And, *'Strengthen yourself and all will be revealed.'* She raised her hands and made an exasperated noise. "Completely. Fucking. Unhelpful. But who am I to talk?" She smacked at the book open on her desk. "So far, the sum total of my usefulness has been to send you on multiple fact-finding missions that have given us very few facts."

"We've learned much thanks to you."

"Not enough." She jabbed her finger at the chronometer. "28 days! That's all we've got. How are we going to find what we need in 28 days when five months hasn't been enough?"

He cupped her face, thumbs stroking her cheeks. "You need to calm down, Rinna." His hands slid down her arms to cup her hands, holding them up so she could see the orange power sparking at her fingertips.

"Shit." Magic sparked out as she moved away from Tam, backing up as quickly as she could to put some distance between them – and the priceless books on the desks and in the stacks nearby. Desperately, she tried to control the unbidden power, but it wouldn't dissipate. This was a big part of the problem. And she worried that even if they did find a way to channel their powers together safely, she wouldn't be able to control hers and then ... boom!

"Breathe, Rinna." Tam followed her, reaching for her hands.

"No. Don't touch. I might hurt you."

"You won't do that."

"I could."

"You won't. I'm certain of it. Just breathe. Your power is simply responding to your emotions. Mine does the same now it doesn't have my cupid power to temper it. Just calm down and everything will be okay."

"I *am* calm!"

He gave her a look.

Hells. He was right. She was behaving like a bloody novice.

"Given you haven't used your power for 2,000 years, it's only natural you'd be a bit rusty," Tam said softly, jumping to the conclusion she let everyone else jump to. "Especially given how quickly it's growing. You're stronger now than when we last faced Clodia."

"So are you – and you're not struggling."

He snorted. "I wouldn't say that." Before she could argue with him over that patently untrue statement, he put his finger on her lips. "You need to give yourself a break. We all think you're doing amazingly well and I'm confident both of us will be ready to do what must be done when the time comes."

"But we still don't know how we're supposed to use these greatly strengthened powers."

"We'll figure it out. It'll be fine. The HBG agrees with me."

It made her smile, his nickname for the HeartsBlood Gem. Only he would give a nickname to something so powerful. "How can you be so certain?"

"Why else would she have picked us to free her after the thousands of years she's been locked away?"

"Because we're just that kind of lucky?" she said, grimacing.

He chuckled and squeezed her hands. "No, because we're the ones she's been waiting for. We're destined to do it."

"I can't believe after all this, you're so keen to embrace this as destiny. You know destiny simply means we have no choice."

"Only if you view the path destiny chose for us as the only choice. I like to think of it more like my cupid arrows –

I might have aimed them at potential lovers to make them notice each other, but what they do after that is their own choice. Destiny is only the path – it is up to us to decide how we walk it." He held up her hands. "And see, I'm right – you can do this."

The power no longer sparked on her fingers. She pursed her lips. "Don't be so smug about it."

"It's not smugness but certainty. I have faith in you. Faith in us. I know we will figure it out."

"How can you be so sure?"

He tugged her closer. The gem that was embedded in his chest glowed as their joint hands hovered over it. Warmth fizzled through her, alongside a sensation of rightness. "Because of this. There is a reason the three of us came together. Only all of us working as one can defeat Clodia. I know it deep in my soul. Don't you?"

She looked into his beautiful indigo eyes – that curiously had not changed colour when his cupid power had been taken – and wished, not for the first time, she had his faith. But he didn't know what she knew. That she was the weak link and if she didn't find some way of changing that, they'd lose.

She stared at him, chewing on her lip. She wanted to tell him. Wanted his help, his advice, but ... she couldn't worry him with this. So instead, she squeezed his fingers and said, "Okay."

"Okay what?"

"You better go. But first, kiss me again." He kissed her lightly on the nose, making her giggle. "I didn't mean like that."

He leaned back, eyes full of his love for her, and not a little mischief. "I hope your research is fruitful, my love. At least you've got the library to yourself for a while. Violetta just sent Jules a message this morning saying she won't be back today as promised – she's found another lead."

"I hope it's more useful than the last one. I could really use her help going through some of the older magical texts. Jules is great, but because of her old magical affliction, she doesn't know the older grimoires as well as Violetta."

"I know, but she had a 'knowing' and there's no talking her out of it. So, she won't be back today and Jules and Bas won't be back until this evening. They're seeing the OBGYN and then having a 'date night'. Except, it's during the day."

"Maybe we can have one of those when you get back."

"Promises, promises." He hauled her against him, kissing her hard and long. She melted into him, giving in to the pull of him, to the incredible desire that raced through her every nerve, muscle and bone, firing a desperate need inside to lose herself in the wonder of what she shared only with him. But thankfully – because they were running out of time – he broke the kiss before she sank too deep.

Panting, he said against her lips, "Stop worrying."

"I'm not."

"You can't fool me," he said, touching his chest above his heart. "I feel your worry."

She knew he could – which made it worse. She didn't want it standing between them and complete happiness; like the kind his parents shared. "I promise to stop worrying if you promise to stop worrying about me."

He chuckled. "Only you could ask the impossible and make it sound reasonable."

"I'm a worrier. You'll just have to get used to it."

"And I am happy to, as long as we share the burden. We both had to rely on ourselves for far too long, but neither of us have to take on everything alone anymore. We have each other. Okay?"

Her mouth twisted but she hid it with a nod. She wanted to share everything with him – Gods how she wanted that – but she just couldn't.

He bent down and pressed a sweet kiss to her lips. "I love you."

"I love you too."

He kissed her again then walked over to the free space between the kitchen and desks, opened a portal and stepped through.

Air displaced as the portal closed, ruffling the papers on the desks around her and cooling her hot face.

Hells! She had to do something soon or he'd begin to suspect exactly how dangerous her growing power was and how little control over it she really had. And she couldn't let him know that. The evil witch-bitch Clodia would break out of her prison in the Void using the rising power of Ostara and the magics she'd stolen, but the HBG assured them they would defeat her, melding their powers together with the spirit in the gem once they'd freed her. Korinna couldn't see how, given how things were right now, but Tam believed implicitly, and it was his total faith in what the HBG had told them that was holding them all up right now. Without it, everything could fall apart. The problem was, unless she did something drastic, that melding of their powers would end in pain and disaster and death.

Her track record spoke for itself after all.

If it was up to her, she'd step away and let Violetta or Bas take her place, but unfortunately, it didn't work that way. According to the HBG, she could only be freed with the active powers of two incredibly powerful magic-users who were bound soul and mind.

Not only that, but from everything they'd discovered – pitifully little – she was key in the HBG's plan not simply because of the strength of her magic and how it worked but because she was the only one amongst them who had torn open the fabric of space and time and gained access to the Void – even though that had been a horrible accident. The only other person who had done it that they knew of was Jules, when she'd torn open the Void and pushed Clodia in there over a year ago. Unfortunately, Jules had thrown all of her power at Clodia to do so, so she couldn't be the one who did it now.

So she was locked into this with no way out.

Which meant going behind Tam's back.

She rubbed her chest at the ache that thought caused. But there was no other option. The only spell she'd ever heard of that could give her the control she needed was in the Eleusinian Mysteries Grimoire – and Persephone had made him vow not to let her see the grimoire as he'd once promised. Thankfully, she'd not made Korinna vow not to go looking for it – she'd just made Tam go back on his promise. Not that she blamed him for that – he couldn't deny a Goddess, not to mention making the vow had meant he could keep the grimoire to use as a resource in the fight ahead. But still, it sucked that this was what it all led to – her sneaking around to take a peek at a grimoire that had been promised to her.

Bloody Persephone. She'd railed at Seph to change her mind, but the Goddess had been adamant.

"Oh, my love. If only you had been truthful with me all these years, this wouldn't be an issue. But how can I trust you with the Mysteries when, at your own admission, you sought to use the soul-transference spell? A spell you know would lead to your death."

"But it was to save the souls I caused to be lost in the Void."

Persephone cupped her face. "Your soul holds far greater

value to me than all those souls put together. As does your life. Tamuel agrees."

"No, he doesn't. He knows I wouldn't use that spell now. Not if using it would hurt him. I would never hurt him. He's my soulmate."

"You would sacrifice yourself to save him."

"I would."

"Then I cannot trust you with that spell."

"What if I promise not to look for it?"

Persephone shook her head slowly. "You think I have forgotten you have an eidetic memory? One glance and you would be able to use it. So no, I cannot allow you to see the grimoire. But because you may need some of what is inside it to help fight Clodia, I have allowed Tamuel to keep it. You must be happy with that for now because it is all I can offer."

It was pointless fighting with the Goddess any further – Seph was one of the most stubborn people Korinna knew, and that was saying something.

So, she'd tried hard to find an alternative. But it was no use. And given she was finally alone for the rest of the day, she had to make her move now.

She had to break into Tam's secret hiding place and steal what had been forbidden to her.

She only hoped that when Tam found out – and she had no doubt eventually he would – he'd understand her decision and forgive her. Because if her soulmate didn't forgive her, she had no idea how she'd live with herself.

～

I hope you enjoyed that sneak peek of ***Blood Cursed***. If you want to read more, you can get your copy here:

https://books2read.com/u/bW6N0G

BEFORE YOU GO, I want to offer you a little something special and FREE ... a prequel novel called *Fractured Curse* about when Korinna and Tamuel first met and what happened to them at the Amazonian training camp.

Turn the page to find out how you get your hands on your FREE prequel novel ...

LOVE A FREE BOOK?

YOUR FREE BOOK IS WAITING

Cursed to never be loved; fated to never be alone ...

Cursed cupid Tamuel has been told he will never love or be loved, a fate to which he's long been resigned. Yet from the moment he meets powerful trainee witch Korinna Soteira at the Amazonian and Gargarean training camp, he knows this to be a lie – he loves Korinna like he's loved nothing and no-one in his life. But his curse is right in one respect: he may be able to love, but he can never *be* loved. Korinna will only ever be his friend, a fact he has spent the last twenty years coming to terms with.

However, malignant forces are stirring in the darkest reaches of the Realms. They have plans to use Korinna and her unusual powers – plans that can only be thwarted by the cursed cupid and an impossible love. Yet breaking

Tamuel's curse now could release a force too ancient to destroy – and thus destroy any future.

What if the only way to survive the present is to place the future in peril?

Fractured Curse is a prequel novella to my popular Gods Cursed Series centring on unknown history between two of readers' favourite characters from the series. It takes place 2000 years before the events in *Love Cursed* and can be read as an introduction into the world or at any time during the reading of the series.

It's exclusive to my newsletter subscribers, so to get your copy, just follow the QR code or link below, fill in your details and it will be winging its way to you along with other free reads, deals and bookish info.

Get My Free Copy of Fractured Curse Here:
https://www.subscribepage.com/fracturedcurse_signup

JOIN LEISL'S LEGENDS

Subscribe to (or follow) me (via the QR code) at my Leisl's Legends page on REAM—a new subscription app like Patreon except it's designed especially for readers and authors for an amazing reading experience— and you will get early access to  *The Huntress and the Vampire King*, my hot enemies to lovers, witch-and-vampire-licious urban fantasy romance that readers over there are already in love with. It's the prequel novel to the first book in the Blood-Rites Series - *The Blood of the Seer*. Be the first to find out where it all began with Anita and Hei's love story.

You will also get exclusive early access to the next book

in the **Gods Cursed Series** and can comment on the story as I write it! Your feedback could be essential in shaping the next book in the series.

Be part of creating the stories you love AND get exclusive access to a whole range of goodies including other WIPs, bonus content, voting rights, signed books and much, much more.

BECOME A LEGEND NOW!
https://reamstories.com/leislleightonauthor

THE HUNTRESS AND THE VAMPIRE KING

She hates the vampire who saved her; he holds the key to her fate ...

Hunter-witch Anita Middleton wants revenge against the violent vampire cults that murdered her father and has worked hard to become one of the best vampire hunters there is. But on a difficult hunt she is caught in an ambush and is mortally wounded ... only to be saved by a mysterious warrior. A warrior with brilliant blue eyes and long silver-blonde hair who fights with a grace and violence like nothing she's seen. It is only after she wakes in the heart of his palazzo that she realises her saviour is a vampire - and according to her brother and mentor, this vampire king is their ally.

Lord Hei rules over an empire of witches, humans and vampires who have been trying to keep the vicious vampire cults, the Wild and Dark Brethren, at bay for centuries. Then he saves Anita and knows with one look she is the prophecied Huntress who could be his downfall or his salvation - and she is also his fated mate. But she struggles to trust him as her hatred of vampires is deep-seated. And she *needs* to trust him because only he can offer the specialised training a Huntress needs so her power won't overwhelm her.

But with the Dark Brethren mysteriously amassing, he has little time to win her over. And Anita must go on a crash course to learn how to control her Huntress magic ... or go slowly and violently insane.

The Huntress and the Vampire King is the exciting action-packed prequel novel to *The Blood of the Seer*.

If you love your vampires hot with a bit of The Witcher thrown in and your heroines as kick-arse as Buffy and even more tortured, if you love fated mates, enemies to lovers, chosen ones and epically hot  **romance mixed with action and mystery, then *The Huntress and the Vampire King* is what you've been waiting for.**

Sign up to Leisl's Legends (via the QR code above) and start reading exclusive early release chapters of it now!

Also by Leisl Leighton

Gods Cursed Series

A Love Cursed Christmas Wish

Love Cursed

Soul Cursed

Blood Cursed

Hearts Cursed

Fates Cursed

Witch Cursed

Dragon Cursed

(Coming 2026)

Blood-Rites Series

The Blood of the Seer

The Blood of the Sire

The Blood of the Son

(Coming 2027)

Blood-Rites Prequel and Bonus Material

The Huntress and the Vampire King

The Middleton Manifesto

(Available now via Leisl's Legends subscription)

PACK BOUND SERIES

Pack Bound

Moon Bound

Shifter Bound

Wolf Bound

Witch Bound

(A Pack Bound Series Prequel Novella)

BOX SET

Pack Bound Series Collection Books 1-4

DAWN OF THE CURSE

A PACK BOUND PREQUEL SERIES

Soul Bound

Alpha Bound

Hunter Bound

Fae Bound

(Coming in 2027)

ANTHOLOGIES

A Perfectly Paranormal Valentine

A Perfectly Paranormal Halloween

A Perfectly Paranormal Easter

A Perfectly Paranormal Christmas

A Perfectly Paranormal Prophecy

(Coming in 2027)

∾

As well as writing sexy, epic and romantic paranormal novels, I write mysterious and emotional romantic suspense novels too. Check out the following titles for amazing, suspenseful reads:

STORM HAVEN SERIES

Need You Tonight

The Devil Inside

∾

COALCLIFF STUD SERIES

Climbing Fear: Book 1

Blazing Fear: Book 2

∾

ECHO SPRINGS SERIES

Dangerous Echoes: Book 1

Books 2-4 in this series, (written by Daniel deLorne, TJ Hamilton and Shannon Curtis) are also available now at all ebook retailers.

About Leisl

Leisl Leighton is a tall red head with an overly large imagination. As a child, she identified strongly with Anne of Green Gables, and like Anne, is a voracious reader and born performer.

It came as no surprise when she went on to a career as a performer, script writer, script doctor, stage manager and musical director for cabaret and theatre restaurants.

After starting a family, Leisl stopped performing and began writing the stories plaguing her dreams. She now writes emotional stories mixed with mystery and a little bit of what goes bump in the night.

Her novels have won and placed in writing contests here and overseas. She is a passionate advocate for the romance genre, was President of Romance Writers of Australia from 2014-2017 and when she's not writing romantic stories of  redemption, she is helping other authors reach their dreams with her Author Services. You can contact Leisl through her website via the QR Code above or here: https://www.leislleighton.com

 And if you want to stay in touch and be the first to find out about new releases, appearances, special deals and exclusive content and giveaways, sign up to her Newsletter and pick up your free copy of *Fractured Curse* via the QR code.

Or sign up to *Leisl's Legends* via this QR code to get *Fractured Curse* plus serialised early access stories and bonus content including a bonus NSFW ending for Love Cursed.

You can also follow her on social media:

- facebook.com/LeislLeightonAuthor
- instagram.com/leislleightonauthor
- BB bookbub.com/authors/leisl-leighton
- a amazon.com/stores/Leisl-Leighton/author/B00DBYRGZY

Acknowledgments

Thanks go to all the usual people: my hubby (the love of my life) and my boys (the other loves of my life); my mum and dad; my sister, brother and their families; my writing group friends—Anita, Marnie, Chris, Laura, Frana—I could do none of this without your love and support through the good and bad (especially in this last few terrible years). You give me the strength to keep going and the room to keep filling my creative well.

Thanks to Helen and Liz—your counsel and amazing friendships will always be missed but what you brought to my life will never be forgotten

Thanks to my agent, Alex Adsett, for encouraging me to go off and pursue getting these stories out there myself.

Thanks once again to my editor, Marnie St Clair—working with you is always a joy.

Thanks to Samantha Marshall for your amazing cover.

And a big thanks to my fellow A Perfectly Paranormal writers – this would not have been written without you. I'll be eternally grateful that you thought of me when coming up with the idea for the anthologies for which this series idea was spawned. It is exciting that this story will live on both in the anthology but also as its own little can-do novel.

Finally, thanks to all the readers. I love writing my stories but it makes it all the more special to know you're right there with me enjoying my characters' trials, joys and general shenanigans right along with me. I hope my stories lift you up and give you all the feels because then my job is done.